BANISHED

THE 3RD FREAK HOUSE TRILOGY, BOOK #2

C.J. ARCHER

WWW.CJARCHER.COM

CHAPTER 1

Hertfordshire, Summer 1889

Frakingham House had never looked less freakish. Light blazed from every one of its windows and from the lamps lining both sides of the front steps. The shadows had been banished, and the recent terrifying events forgotten, albeit temporarily. A steady stream of grand coaches led by handsome pairs of matching horses deposited gentlemen and ladies before heading around to the stables. The hats and glittering tiaras tilted back as the guests peered up at the usually somber façade of the house and passed judgment. It was the first time most had seen the infamous mansion.

Whether their opinions were favorable or not, I didn't know. I was too far away to hear, seated as I was in the music room. I turned away from the window and instead stared at the empty space in the middle of the room where the piano usually stood. It had been carried upstairs to the ballroom for the evening, where the pianist was currently playing a gentle sonata as Sylvia Langley greeted her guests alongside her cousin and his new wife. The music room seemed wrong without its main focus. Not only empty, but pointless. It was now just another room in a house full of them.

"There you are," said Emily, sailing gracefully through the door like a boat across the smooth surface of a lake. "I've been instructed to fetch you and march you upstairs whether you want to go or not."

"By Sylvia?"

"Goodness, no. She's too excited to notice your absence. My instructions came from Hannah and Charity."

"That's sweet of them," I said, absently.

"I was coming to look for you anyway." Emily's smile faded and her dark eyes softened. The time for forced cheerfulness was over, on her part, at least. "Are you all right, Cara?"

"Of course. I was a little overwhelmed and needed some time to myself, that's all. There are so many grand personages in the ballroom that I'm quite giddy from switching my gaze between them all."

Her lips twitched, despite her frown. "You might fool Sylvia with that little speech, but not me. I doubt you even know who any of the guests are."

"I do! I saw that dreadful woman arrive with her odious son."

"Which one?"

Clearly I'd met so many dreadful women with odious sons since my return to England that not even my niece could remember them all. "The one whom you foisted upon me at some soiree or other. She talked about how wonderful her son was all evening, yet he couldn't stop looking at my chest."

"Be thankful he even noticed your chest, flat as it is."

That finally coaxed a genuine smile from me, making Emily grin back. "Oh, and Mr. and Mrs. Butterworth from the village are here," I went on. "I think she's the only person more excited than Sylvia tonight. So many eligible gentlemen to dangle her silly daughters in front of! Which ones will take the bait?"

"Which ones deserve the twin twits?"

"Far too many to count."

"Now, now. There are some young gentlemen in there who are quite pleasant to talk to."

I rolled my eyes. "Pleasant? Good lord, Emily, you make them sound so dull. Please, stop me from throwing myself at all those pleasant men!"

She gave me a withering glare. "That isn't fair. I'm only trying to take your mind off—" She pressed her lips together and looked away.

"You can say his name, Em. Quin. Quintin St. Clair." I spat it out, challenging her, but I wasn't quite sure why. "And I do not have him on my mind."

"No? Then why did you assume he was the one I was about to mention?" Her hand on hip posture was a challenge to *me*.

I would not rise to it. Indeed, I said nothing and stood, turning to watch through the window as one of the footmen opened a coach door for two new arrivals.

Behind me, Emily sighed. "I know why you're hiding away in here."

"I'm not hiding."

"And I don't blame you in the least," she went on as if I hadn't spoken. "You miss him."

"I don't."

"I am sympathetic. But you must come back to the ballroom. Not only for Sylvia's sake, or Charity and Hannah's, but for mine."

I squared up to her. "Yours?"

"I'm worried about you." She looped her arm through

mine and fixed me with those brown eyes of hers that were incongruously soft, yet determined too. She wasn't going to surrender easily. "In the three weeks since you were last here at Frakingham, you've hardly been anywhere or done anything. You won't go visiting with me or receive callers. You wouldn't even come shopping."

She *was* worried. It was etched into every new line around her mouth and the way she looked at me, as if she expected me to burst into tears. I had, but not in company. Since leaving Frakingham, three weeks prior, I'd been listless, unable to concentrate on tasks and disinterested in the world around me. I'd hardly smiled and never laughed. Emily was right. I missed Quin.

But missing Quin was a pointless exercise. Even if he came back to this realm, he was dead anyway, destined to return to Purgatory. I might have liked kissing him and being with him, but I wasn't fool enough to dream that there could be more.

It was easy to tell myself that. Much, much harder to get my heart to listen.

"Come on," I said, steering her toward the door. "Let's see which gentlemen have fallen into Mrs. Butterworth's trap."

"And then we shall see which ones fall into mine."

I groaned. "It's going to be a long night."

We headed up the stairs and rejoined Sylvia and the others. As August Langley's niece, she had been mistress at Frakingham for the last eight years, despite not even being twenty yet. But now that her cousin had married, she was destined to take a back seat to Hannah Langley. She claimed not to mind, but watching her hosting her first ball, I wondered if she would continue to be so gracious.

She smiled at all her guests and made a point of engaging them in conversation. Her behavior could have been taken straight from the handbook on hostessing. She made everyone in that room seem like they mattered, even the wallflowers sitting on the chairs at the edge of the dance floor. I noticed her nudge Jack and Samuel toward them on more than one occasion.

"She's quite the *tour de force* when she wants to be," said Hannah, sidling up to me. Her red hair was bound in a loose style that was all the rage in Paris, apparently, allowing some of her curls to hang free around her pretty face. She wore a lovely deep green gown with rosettes and lace at the bodice and along the hemline. It suited her perfectly.

"I admit to being very impressed with Sylvia's handling of tonight," I said. "The evening has run smoothly so far, and the guests seem charmed by her."

"They do, and I admit to being somewhat surprised that it has turned out so well. It wasn't that long ago that the mere thought of throwing a ball would send Sylvia into fits of anxiety."

"She told me she hasn't slept in three weeks."

Hannah smiled. "I can vouch for the truth in that. I heard her pacing up and down the hallway one night."

"Are you sure she wasn't visiting Tommy on the sly?"

Her smile widened. "If she was, then nothing has come of it. He complained to Jack that he's hardly seen her lately."

"Poor Tommy." My heart felt heavier at the thought of him, although I hadn't seen him since my arrival yesterday. According to Jack and Hannah, Tommy's arm was still bandaged from when he'd injured it fighting off an army of demons alongside Quin.

"Don't worry too much about him," she said. "He's been busy teaching the new servants what to do, and barking orders left and right in preparation for tonight, much to Bradford's displeasure."

Bradford was the new butler who'd taken up the position mere weeks ago. It would seem the power struggle between

Tommy and Bradford was destined to continue, despite Tommy's incapacity.

"And what happens when tonight is over and the servants no longer need directing?"

"We must hope that Tommy is willing to take on a new role. One that doesn't require him to use both arms."

"One that involves Sylvia?"

We both watched her as she flitted through to the refreshment room like a butterfly between roses.

"I'm not so sure that she wants to be involved," Hannah said.

She did seem to have forgotten all about Tommy, despite showing signs of affection for him earlier. Perhaps having Jack and Hannah home had put things into perspective for her, or perhaps her uncle had made it clear he didn't condone the relationship—if he knew about it at all, that is.

I was about to ask Hannah when Charity and Samuel joined us. They'd been inseparable most of the night, except for when Samuel had obliged Sylvia by dancing with the odd girl, here and there. I was struck again by how dazzling they were as a couple. Both tall, blonde and strikingly beautiful, they were a match in looks as well as sensibility. He was charming and she was somewhat reserved, although I'd seen how fierce she could be when necessary. Like Jacob, Emily and myself, they had arrived at Frakingham yesterday and would stay overnight while the rest of the guests drove back to the village or to other houses nearby. Securing accommodation for everyone had been quite a feat for Sylvia. She really had surpassed my expectations.

"Have you seen who's here?" Samuel asked me.

I scanned the guests milling behind him and seeing nobody I knew, shrugged. "Who?"

"Faraday."

"Nathaniel!" I looked again, but still didn't spot him. "What's he doing here?"

The last time I'd seen Nathaniel Faraday was in Harborough, just before Quin had left this realm three weeks ago. He'd been with Everett Myer, the master of the Society for Supernatural Activity, and they'd been after the same ancient book of spells as us. We'd reached it first, thanks only to Nathaniel delaying Myer in London. I wasn't yet sure whether to trust him or not. I certainly didn't trust Myer, and if Nathaniel continued to assist him, it would seem I couldn't trust him either. It was a pity, because I'd enjoyed his company when I'd first met him on the long voyage from the colony of Victoria on the S.S. Bombay. At the time, I'd wanted to get to know him better. Now, I felt about him in much the same way I felt about most gentlemen I'd met in England—ambivalent.

"I think Sylvia invited him," Charity told me, also scanning the guests standing at the edges of the ballroom.

"Why would she do that?"

Three pairs of eyes looked at me as if I were a fool.

"Oh." I felt my cheeks burn, and I wished they wouldn't, since I no longer thought of Nathaniel in *that* way. "Well. You do all know that he cannot be completely trusted, don't you?"

They nodded.

"And that he may be on Myer's side."

"We know," Charity said gently, taking my hand and squeezing it. "But he also may not be. Emily told us how he failed to tell Myer where to find the book until it was too late."

Hannah took my other hand. "So much has happened here in our absence. I must say, it's been a busy spring."

"But you're back now," I said with the cheerfulness I knew they all hoped to hear. "Frakingham will resume its normal routine again and all will be well."

"Yes," Hannah said, searching the crowd. Her gaze rested on a tall, dark-haired figure striding toward us. She smiled then walked off to meet her husband.

"He's coming," Charity whispered in my ear before she and Samuel melted into the crowd.

I thought she meant Jack Langley until I saw Nathaniel splitting off from a group of gentlemen and heading my way. I was torn between pretending to see someone I wanted to speak to and greeting him like an old friend. My indecision meant I remained rooted to the floor and an easy target.

"Good evening, Cara." He bowed smoothly, sending his sandy curls tumbling forward over his eyes, where they remained after he straightened. They did not hide the way his gaze roamed down my length, however, or lingered on my mouth. "You're looking particularly handsome tonight."

Handsome? That was the best he could do? Apparently not, because he continued on. And on.

"That shade of pink is particularly pleasing for a girl of your coloring. And the beading around the neckline and in your hair sparkles in this light. Indeed, the ones in your hair are like stars in the darkest night sky. You should be commended on your choice of gown and accessories tonight." His chortle didn't suit a gentleman with such a lean frame and handsome face. It belonged on someone more robust and older. "Listen to me. I've become quite the fashion critic. My friends would laugh to hear me talk to a pretty young girl in such a manner, but I just can't help myself."

"Indeed. Excuse me, Nathaniel, but I must find my niece and her husband." I wasn't usually so dismissive of a gentleman's attempts at flattery. It was rare enough that I was ordinarily pleased to receive any and all compliments. But tonight, and for the last three weeks, my tolerance had sunk low and my patience worn thin. Even so, Nathaniel's crestfallen face gave me pause. I offered him a smile and my hand.

He kissed it with dry lips. "Forgive me, Nathaniel. I'm out of sorts lately."

"That's quite all right. I suppose it's been an odd time for you, what with that fellow from Purgatory clinging to you and learning of my involvement with Myer."

"He didn't cling. He saved my life, more than once."

"How? Was there a demon infestation? Or something else related to the portal here at Frakingham?"

I hadn't told him about the curse that had been inflicted upon me, and Quin's role in keeping me alive while we hunted down the book that contained the counter curse. Nathaniel had worked out that Quin was from Purgatory, but had not told Myer, something for which I was grateful. Nathaniel seemed the less inquisitive of the two, preferring to avoid Quin, after he discovered the truth about him, rather than pepper him with questions.

Or so I'd thought.

"Tell me, what was he like?"

I shrugged one shoulder, causing the strip of silk there to slip down and reveal more skin. Nathaniel didn't seem to notice, intent as he was on my mouth as he waited for my answer. "Quin was a gentleman and a warrior, with the traits of both," I told him.

"I see. Was he old?"

"Very."

"And how did he get into Purgatory?"

"He didn't say."

"Didn't or wouldn't?"

"I'm not sure."

He leaned in closer. "Did you summon him or did he simply appear?"

"I summoned him."

"Did he happen to mention what Purgatory is like?"

"These are quite a lot of questions, Nathaniel. A lady might think you were only talking to her to get answers."

His face reddened. "I, er, my apologies, Cara. I didn't mean to offend."

"I'm not offended, but I am curious as to why you're asking these questions of me now, when you could have asked Quin when he was here. Instead, you ran away."

He stroked his jacket lapels, brushing off lint that wasn't there. "I admit his presence was somewhat..."

"Intimidating?"

"Overwhelming."

"I see. Tell me, Nathaniel, are you still assisting Mr. Myer with his research now that the book has been found?"

"I am not entirely sure what the future holds in that regard."

We had told Nathaniel and Myer that Quin had hidden the book without telling us where, but it was doubtful that Nathaniel believed that, considering he knew Quin was a warrior from Purgatory. Myer, however, did not know and quite likely believed our story. In truth, *Samuel* had hidden the book and not told any of us. He was the only one immune to Myer's hypnosis and therefore the only one who could keep the location safe. We hadn't heard from Myer since Quin left but I was in no doubt that he hadn't given up the search. He was obsessed with obtaining the book and keeping the portal at Frakingham Abbey open, despite the dangers that could be summoned through it.

The music changed to a waltz and more people flowed onto the dance floor in waves of silk and perfume. Nathaniel bowed to me. "Will you do me the honor of dancing with me, Cara?"

My dance card was entirely empty since I had spoken to so few gentlemen thus far. I had no grounds on which to refuse him, and doing so would be terribly poor manners.

Besides, Nathaniel had proven to be a thoroughly interesting conversationalist, as long as we steered away from discussions of Myer, magical books and Quin. I thought it safe to assume we'd exhausted those topics.

"Of course." I put out my hand and he beamed as he led me onto the dance floor.

We took a few moments to find our rhythm, but once we did, he resumed the conversation about paranormal matters. I instantly regretted my decision to dance with him.

"Nathaniel," I said, interrupting his question about spirits and what they look like to we mediums. "Do you think we can have a conversation that does not involve ghosts, ecto-plasm, demons, other realms, or spells?"

He blinked owlishly at me. "Oh. What topic would you like to discuss?"

"I don't care, but we used to talk about a great many things on the journey from Melbourne." I hadn't even known he was a paranormal historian until meeting him again in London. It hadn't come up on the ship.

It would seem he couldn't think of a single thing and we finished the rest of the dance in silence. When the music ended, he politely bowed and walked away. I headed in the opposite direction, feeling somewhat bruised. It would seem Nathaniel only enjoyed my company these days when the paranormal was a topic.

"Good evening." The mumbled, sluggish voice halted me in my path. "It's Miss Moreau, isn't it?"

My heart plunged and I forced myself to turn with a smile plastered to my face. "Lord Alwyn," I said, giving the giant gentleman a shallow curtsy. "I'm surprised to see you here." Particularly since he wasn't on the guest list. I ought to know; I'd helped Sylvia draw it up.

His wide, fleshy lips stretched around the cigar that was perpetually perched between them, despite the ballroom not being the place for such smelly things. I think he was smiling at me, but it was difficult to tell. I forced a smile anyway.

"Lady Alwyn and I are delighted to have been invited to this fine house," he said with a thrust of his considerable girth. The man was very tall and broadly built. In his youth, he probably cut a fine, strong figure, but in middle age, the muscle had run to fat, his hair was thinning, and the skin on his face had slackened and sagged. "I must say you're looking somewhat prettier than the last time we met."

Considering the last time we'd met I'd been dressed as a boy, it wasn't much of a compliment. Byron Mordant-Turpin, the eighth earl of Alwyn, had forced Quin to fight in an illegal boxing match before he would tell us who had bought many of the books from his library, including the book of spells that would cure me. He was a notorious gambler, liar, cheat, and a generally unpleasant fellow who'd backed us into a difficult corner, getting us in trouble with the organizer of the bare knuckle fights, a nasty ruffian by the name of Bains.

"Shall we dance, Miss Moreau?" he asked as the music changed again.

Dancing with him meant touching him. *Ugh.* "I regret that my card is full."

"Come now, there's no need to lie." He chomped down on his cigar, dropping ash onto his jacket. "I've been watching you, Miss Moreau, and I know your card is empty. Fellows prefer English roses to African exotics. You need to make your connection to Beaufort better known if you want to make 'em flock."

"Do you usually insult the ladies you ask to dance?"

He held out his hand. "I only want to waltz with a pretty young lady. There's nothing sinister in that, eh?"

I glanced around, but saw nobody I knew. Rescue would

not be forthcoming. "Put out your cigar first. I don't want ash in my hair."

He chuckled and did as I asked, stabbing the butt on the back of a nearby chair and flinging it into the corner. I pulled a face at his back and steeled myself for a horrid few minutes.

He led me onto the dance floor and we took up our positions. I stood as far from him as I could while still performing the waltz, but his stomach was so large that I kept bumping against it.

"Suppose you're wondering why I'm here," he said.

"Not particularly."

"You are, you just don't want to admit it." Even without the cigar in his mouth, he still mumbled his words. "I made some enquiries about you and your friend, St. Clair."

I held my breath and hazarded a glance up at him. "And what did you learn?"

"I learned that St. Clair has returned to Melbourne, and I already knew more about him than anyone else I spoke with. He's quite the mystery man."

I blew out the breath and relaxed a little. It would seem Alwyn wasn't aware of Quin's supernatural existence. Hopefully he wasn't aware of the supernatural at all.

"I also learned that you're friendly with the Langley girl. My wife mentioned this ball and we took the liberty of turning up tonight, since Miss Langley's invitation must have been mislaid." The grin he gave me was wolfish.

"Is there a point you're trying to make, my lord?"

"Well, well, aren't you the inquisitive one? I should have guessed, considering the circumstances in which we first met." His grip tightened on my hand and waist, trapping me. "You're a fortunate woman, Miss Moreau. I don't dance with just anyone these days." He leaned down until his mouth was near my ear. His hot breath fanned my hair. "I also don't like being lied to."

I would not be intimidated by this man, particularly in a room full of people. He couldn't do anything to me here. "Are you referring to me being dressed as a boy at The Brickmaker's Arms? Because I assure you, that had nothing to do with duping you and everything to do with me wanting an adventure. When did you realize I was a girl?"

"Almost immediately. I thought it safer to keep your secret. Not sure what all those brutes would have done to a pretty chit like you if they'd sniffed out some sport."

"Thank you. I think." His words didn't particularly worry me. I'd had Quin to keep me safe at the time. I certainly wouldn't have entered into such a place without him there to protect me.

"What is it you want, sir? I doubt you came all this way just to dance, and there's little sport to be had here in sleepy Hertfordshire."

"I'm not here for sport, I'm here for answers. I want to know why my book was so important to you and St. Clair."

"Quin is a historian and the book was one he needed for his research."

He swung me about a little more violently than the dance necessitated. "Don't lie to me, girl," he snarled, baring large teeth. "You'll find I make a very unpleasant enemy."

I swallowed. My thoughts raced, even as my stomach dove. Telling him about the book risked too much. He might not have an interest in the paranormal now, but if he knew the book's value and power, I suspected he would suddenly develop one. But this man was astute and would know if I lied.

"It was just a book, my lord," I said in the strongest voice I could muster. "You would need to ask Mr. St. Clair what was in it. I barely glanced at it."

"No. No, no, no." His grip on my hand became bruising. I winced and tried to pull free, but that only brought more pain shooting into my wrists. "You see, some days after I last saw you, I began to ponder about the book and the vast distance Mr. St. Clair had traveled to find it. It was his nature that first set off alarm bells. You see, he's not the bookish type. Not in the least. So why did he want to read the books in my library? When I could also find out nothing about him, I began to wonder. I spoke to the priest who'd brokered the purchase, and he told me about the bookseller. He in turn told me about yourselves and a certain other gentleman who'd come looking for the book that day. I believe Mr. Faraday is here tonight, but not his employer, Mr. Myer. If Myer had an interest in the particular tome, then I am certainly interested now too." He spoke as quietly as his booming voice allowed. "Because if he wants it, he will pay to get it and not care about the sum. The man is richer than the queen."

"He is that. But I can assure you, I no longer have the book. Quin hid it."

"Perhaps. Or perhaps not. Either way, you're going to get it back for me, Miss Moreau."

He eased his hold and I pulled free and stepped a little away from him, bumping into the couple whirling past. We both stood in the middle of the dance floor as the dancers dipped and swirled around us to the increasing tempo of the music. It was like standing in the eye of a storm, waiting for it to unleash its force upon us. The problem was, I had no anchor, no strong pillar to hold onto. I was alone with an unpredictable and very large man, without any friends or family to keep me safe.

"Why would I do that, sir?" I asked him. It was easy to sound brave. Much harder to feel it. My heart hammered in my chest and my palms felt cold, clammy. "You sold the book and we acquired it from the gentleman who bought it from you." Acquired it under the most violent circumstances that saw Lord Frakingham's heir, Douglas Malborough, die.

"You're not hearing me, Miss Moreau. I don't care that the book has been bought and sold. I want it back. It's my family heirloom." He fished in his inside jacket pocket and pulled out a cigar longer than his finger. "The book belongs in the Alwyn library. For sentimental reasons." He shoved the cigar between his lips and chomped down on it. "I'm sure a girl like you understands the importance of family and history."

If anything sets my blood boiling, it's men like him who think of me as having little more value than an exotic curiosity. "A girl like me?"

He chuckled, apparently finding my hot temper amusing. "A girl who likes her family. A girl with a lot to lose."

Just like that my ire dissolved, replaced by uncertainty again and a sickening sense of dread. "What are you implying?" My small voice was almost lost as the band whipped their playing into a crescendo that had the dancers spinning into a frenzy.

He leaned forward and kept his voice low. "I am a man who gets what he wants. Always. Sometimes I have to use unsavory methods to achieve my ends, but that's only because I find those methods are the currency that get a response. Do not force my hand, Miss Moreau. I don't want to hurt any of your loved ones—but I will." He straightened to his full height and pushed out his barrel chest. He didn't smile, but there was a hard gleam in his eyes that dared me to test him so he could prove what he was capable of. "Do we understand one another, Miss Moreau?"

I nodded quickly. What else could I do? The man was unscrupulous and greedy. Whether he was the sort to follow through on such a horrible threat, I didn't know. Nor did I want to find out. I felt sick as I watched his thick lips spread into a grin.

"I'll be generous and give you four days. If you don't have the book by then..." He bowed and walked off the dance floor as the music died away and the dancers came to a stop.

I ran past them and out of the ballroom, my stomach doing wild flips and my hands shaking. I couldn't think through the dilemma he'd slapped on me, couldn't decide what the best course of action was. All I knew was that I wanted Quin, not simply for his advice and the protection he offered, but to share the burden of the decision that had to be made.

CHAPTER 2

There were too many of us to fit into the smaller drawing room the Langleys preferred to use on a daily basis, so we retreated instead to the more formal one. I had already been on a morning walk with Emily and Jacob, to clear my head and tell them what Lord Alwyn had said, and now it was time to tell the others. Despite its cavernous size, the drawing room seemed crowded with Sylvia, Tommy, August Langley, Bollard, Emily and Jacob Beaufort, Jack and Hannah Langley, Samuel Gladstone and Charity, George and Adelaide Culvert, and myself all assembled.

"How is everyone this morning?" Sylvia said around a yawn. "I do hope you all slept well and enjoyed yourselves last night."

A round of nods and thanks followed, with assurances from everyone that the ball had been a success. Sylvia glowed at the praise.

"Wouldn't you agree, Mr. Langley?" Hannah asked. She sat beside Jack, their hands interlinked, every bit the contented newlyweds.

"Everyone seemed to enjoy themselves," Langley agreed.

He signaled Bollard to wheel him a little further into the room. "There were several interesting gentlemen there."

"And ladies too," Sylvia added.

Her uncle gave her a flat smile. It was clear that he was referring to *eligible* gentlemen, the sort he felt were right for his niece. However, if anyone had paid her particular attention, I hadn't noticed. Then again, I was distracted for much of the evening.

Tommy shifted his stance. We had all insisted he sit, but he'd refused. His bandaged arm was cradled close to his body in a sling, but the other visible signs of the demon attacks had faded on his face and hands. He watched Sylvia from beneath lowered lashes, perhaps to gauge her reaction to her uncle's mention of gentlemen. She gave nothing away. Perhaps she wasn't even aware what Langley had been referring to.

"Did *you* enjoy yourself, Sylvia?" Charity asked her.

"I did." Sylvia chewed on her lower lip and didn't meet anyone's gaze. I raised my eyebrow at Charity, and she lifted one shoulder in a shrug.

"Did anyone see Lord and Lady Alwyn?" Jacob cut in. He'd been agitated ever since I'd told him about my encounter with the earl. He wanted to leave for London immediately, but Emily and I managed to convince him to stay until the following morning in order to discuss Alwyn's threat with the others.

"Alwyn!" George screwed up his nose, but I wasn't sure if it was with displeasure at hearing that Alwyn had attended the ball or to keep his glasses in place. "What was he doing here?"

"That's what I'd like to know," Sylvia said with a sniff. "I didn't invite them, but I couldn't confront them. Or should I have done so?" She returned to chewing her lip. "Did I do the right thing?"

"You did," Emily assured her. "It was terribly bad form, and I'm surprised at Lady Alwyn. She ought not to have committed such a faux pas."

"She may not have had a choice," Jacob told his wife. "If her husband ordered her to come, she would have had to do as he bid."

"But that's the thing," Sylvia whined. "Why would he want to come here? I didn't think he was the sort to care about balls and country parties."

"He doesn't." Jacob looked to me and nodded at me to go on.

"Who's Alwyn?" Jack asked before I could.

"A gentlemen we met recently in London," I told him. "I think he came here to speak to me. Or, rather, threaten me." I launched into the details of my conversation with Alwyn and was met with stunned silence upon completion.

Tommy finally sat and absently rubbed his injured elbow. "Blimey," he muttered.

"Do you think him capable of doing such a thing?" Hannah asked Jacob.

Jacob shrugged. "I don't know the fellow well enough. Cara and I met him briefly while searching for the book. He certainly didn't strike me as a man with many scruples, so it's possible."

"None of us should take the threat lightly," I warned them. "Everyone in this room is linked to me in one way or another. I want you all to be extra vigilant."

"But what will you do?" Charity asked. "Give him the book, or call his bluff, if he is indeed bluffing?"

"We can't give him the book," Langley said. "He'll sell it to Myer and Myer will unleash hell on my doorstep."

Sylvia and Adelaide both whimpered. George patted his wife's arm and she sidled closer to him on the sofa.

"Agreed," Jack said. "The book must remain hidden."

Jacob and Emily exchanged glances and something unspoken passed between them. "None of you have children," he said heavily. "They're the most vulnerable."

Sylvia covered her mouth with her hand. Tommy half rose to go to her, but quickly sat again and fidgeted with his sling instead.

"Then what do you propose we do?" Jack asked. "Sit and wait? Give him the book?"

"We could try tricking him," Adelaide said. "Give him another old book and tell him it's the one."

"That might work, but only until he tries to sell it to Myer. He'll know the difference."

Jacob dragged his hand through his hair and down his face. He looked so tired and I hated that I'd been such trouble to him, to all of them. I knew it wasn't my fault, but I felt the weight of responsibility nevertheless.

"You've all forgotten one obvious answer," Samuel said. To my surprise, he was smiling. And then I realized why.

Charity brightened. "Of course!"

Jack smiled too. "How could we forget?"

George slapped his knee and immense relief passed over Jacob's face, lifting the shadows in his eyes.

"What?" Sylvia asked, glancing between us. "What have we forgotten?"

"I'll hypnotize Alwyn," Samuel said. "Charity and I will return to London on this afternoon's train and I'll seek him out and hypnotize him tonight."

"Can you do it in such a way that he won't be aware that he has been hypnotized?" Emily asked.

"I can. While he's under, I'll tell him to forget about the book entirely. By the time I'm finished, he won't even know of its existence anymore."

It was a huge relief to have the matter resolved, and in

such a simple manner. Even Charity seemed at ease with Samuel using his hypnosis to stop Alwyn.

"Alwyn isn't aware of your ability?" Jack asked.

Samuel shook his head. "As far as we know, he's not aware of anything about the supernatural."

"Except that he does know Myer is master of the society," I added.

"Yes, but he probably thinks Myer and his fellow members are crackpots. I can't see Alwyn being a believer in the paranormal."

"He does seem to lack imagination," Emily said. "And it does require one to set aside practicalities and look at things differently."

It was with a sense of relief that we said goodbye to Samuel and Charity that afternoon, instead of the following morning as planned. I, for one, was anxious to have Alwyn's threat defused as quickly as possible.

After we waved them off, I headed to the library for some peace and quiet. It wasn't until I pulled a particular book from the shelves that I could admit to myself that it wasn't peace and quiet I sought, but information. I settled at the table with the history book and turned to the index first.

The name Quintin St. Clair stared back at me in bold, black lettering. I swallowed. I had been putting off searching through historical texts on the crusades because I wasn't sure I should learn anything more about him. After all, what was the point? It was doubtful if I would see him again, and if I did, nothing could come of it. Besides, researching his life without his knowledge felt wrong, like I was listening to tales behind his back.

I'd finally decided to dispense with that thinking and just do it. Perhaps it was the constant reminder of him, now that I was back in the place where we'd parted. Or perhaps the weight of missing him for three whole weeks had finally worn me down to a point where I would grasp at anything to feel close to him again. Learning about his life through history books was hardly a satisfying way to accomplish that, but it was better than nothing.

I flipped to the page and read the short entry. Quintin St. Clair was born in Essex in 1164 and died in Jaffa, in the Holy Land, in 1191 at the age of twenty-seven. His parents' names weren't listed, and only one of his brothers was mentioned, Guy St. Clair, who also died in 1191 in Jaffa. Quin was knighted in 1189 and had been considered a confidant of King Richard I, known as The Lionheart. He married Maria when he was seventeen, but her last name, age and ancestry had been lost to the mists of time and weren't noted.

That was the total of the known details about Quin's life, summed up in a few pedestrian lines that not even a history student would bother to memorize. It told the reader nothing about the man himself. It didn't mention how he got the scars on his back or how he'd died. It failed to describe his quick temper or his sense of humor, or his insatiable curiosity and fascination with all modern things. It didn't tell me whether his protective streak was all encompassing, or whether it was reserved only for me. It didn't tell me if he'd loved his wife. Maria. Did he think about her, even now? I'd gleaned more answers from the man of mystery himself.

"There you are," said Sylvia, entering the library. "I've been looking for you."

I slammed the book closed, not wanting her to think that I was still preoccupied with Quin, but she didn't even glance at it. She sat in a comfortable chair by the unlit fireplace and plucked at her skirt. Her forlorn sigh had me asking her what the matter was, which I suspected was her intention.

"I want your honest opinion," she said, settling her restless hands in her lap. "Do you think the ball was a success or not?"

"It was, very much so. Why are you unsure? What has been said?"

"Nothing. At least, nothing that I know of. Why, what have you heard?"

"Only good things. So what's brought on this uncertainty?"

Her hands took up their busy work again and she sighed once more. "It's just that...the gentlemen were so..." She shrugged droopy shoulders.

"Dull?"

"Horrid."

"Horrid? In what way? Did one of them say something to you?"

"Not to my face, but I did overhear one of them telling another that I was pretty enough, but far too silly and provincial for his taste."

I dragged my chair over to her side and rested my hand on top of hers. "Sylvia, look at me."

She did. Her eyes were huge and watery.

"I have spent much of my life being the oddity. If my skin color doesn't single me out, the rumors of my medium abilities eventually do. I've been stared and pointed at, ignored, laughed at, sneered at, called a freak, a fraud, a savage, barbarian and worse. In fact, I was called a 'devil's whore' only a few weeks ago. Yes, it hurts—sometimes deeply. Especially when the people I thought were the kindest turn out to be the cruelest. I learned many years ago that those are not the friends I want to gather around me. I don't even want to waste time thinking about them. I have many other things I do want to think about, and people I would prefer to give my time and friendship to. People like you and Charity, Hannah, Emily, Jacob, and other members of my family."

She gave me a weak smile. "I do know all of that, and your

situation has been so much worse than mine. I feel somewhat foolish for bringing it up at all."

"Don't be. Your feelings have been hurt, and you have every right to feel sad about the duplicity of those men. But not for too long. Don't let them upset you for any length of time because they're not worth it. You have other friends who adore you just the way you are."

I thought my speech quite a good one, but she didn't seem any happier. Her brow wrinkled further. "I do appreciate my friends," she assured me. "I know how lucky I am to have such good ones. The problem is, I'm supposed to choose a husband from among one of those toads."

"As am I," I muttered.

"Yet there's not a single one I wanted to spend five minutes with, let alone a lifetime."

"You don't have to choose yet. You have time to meet someone else."

"Uncle August is becoming insistent."

"He is? Why now?"

She sucked in her bottom lip and nibbled it. "I think it may have something to do with Tommy."

"I don't understand. I know Tommy is sweet on you, but he must know that nothing can happen. As do you."

She nibbled more and would not meet my gaze.

"Sylvia? What's happened?"

"Nothing! Nothing like that. It's just that…I may have given Uncle August the impression that Tommy possesses the qualities I would like in a husband." She suddenly grasped my hands, twisting to face me. "He is so much more of a gentleman than any of the ones I danced with last night. He's kind and even-tempered, and he likes me as I am."

I formed an O with my mouth. If I wasn't certain of her feelings for Tommy before, I was now. "So Mr. Langley thinks you wish to marry him?"

She nodded.

"And he's worried that you might run off with the footman and ruin your reputation—and his."

She nodded again.

It was quite the delicious scandal, except it wasn't so delicious when it was happening to a friend. Poor Sylvia looked stricken.

"What does Tommy think?" I asked.

"I haven't told him. I can't speak to him about such a thing. It would be terribly inappropriate."

"Would it? It seems to me that if he has feelings for you, and you have feelings for him, you ought to at least discuss what to do about it. Perhaps he will make a declaration and throw his hat into the ring."

"Make a declaration!" From the look of horror she gave me, one would think I'd suggested she run naked through the streets of Harborough. "Honestly, Cara, I'm surprised at you. I thought you would offer me sage advice, not make it worse."

"I'm sorry you think that way, but I stand by my suggestion. What's wrong with it?"

"I'm looking for a sensible solution to my problem. This is no fairytale, Cara. Tommy and I cannot be together. Uncle would make our lives miserable. He would never let me forget what a poor choice I made, and I'm afraid that would infect all the good in our relationship and turn it sour."

"Then I suggest you beg your uncle to allow you more time to choose a suitable husband."

"He said he has given me enough time. If I haven't chosen by Samuel and Charity's wedding, he's going to choose for me." She pulled a face. "Can you imagine? He'll find me a terribly noble gentleman, with no money to his name, who'll be sweet to my face then look down his nose at me after we're married. It will be positively awful."

I sighed. "Then it seems you have only one course of action to take."

"Yes?" she asked eagerly. "What do you suggest?"

"That you decide if you and Tommy love each other enough to weather the storm that will break over your heads if you choose one another." She opened her mouth to protest, but I held my finger up. "Think about it, Sylvia. Try to imagine the worst thing that could happen if you do choose him. And then try to imagine if you would still love him anyway, and he you. Because you are absolutely right. There are no such things as fairytales. But I, for one, do believe in happy endings. What do you want your happy ending to look like? Could it include Tommy or not if the worst comes to pass?"

I leaned forward and kissed the top of her forehead. When I sat back, I saw that she had a rather stupefied look on her face. I couldn't decipher what it meant, or whether my words had made any impact at all.

"I don't know if that helps or not," I said, "but that's what I would do in your situation."

"Thank you. I think."

"I hope you see that you're lucky, Sylvia. Lucky that your uncle cares enough about you to want the best for you. Lucky in that no matter what happens, Jack and Hannah will never cast you aside. And very lucky that Tommy cares for you as you are."

She blinked at me slowly, as if awaking from a dream, then flung her arms around me, almost knocking me off the chair. "And lucky that my friends are so wonderful."

I smiled. "You might not think so if you follow my advice. It will not be an easy path."

"I'll think about what you've said. I'm not sure what I want yet."

I sighed as she resumed her seat. "Nor am I."

"I'm so sorry. Here I am telling you my problems, when you've got the same pressure from your family."

"Not quite the same. They have allowed me to choose my own husband. Nor do I have to make a decision by the wedding."

"And if you can't choose? If you're presented with someone unsuitable whom you cannot stop thinking about? Will they be so accommodating then?"

I glanced back at the history book on the table. "If it were possible for us to be together, then they would support me." If it were impossible, however, their love and support wouldn't matter.

She sighed once more and slumped back into the chair. "All that organizing and fuss for the ball and I'm right back where I started. I'm not sure it was worth it, in the end."

"You seemed to enjoy yourself though."

"Did I? I don't recall. It's all a blur. It was such terribly hard work, and I hardly knew most of the guests. I know I have Emily to thank for many of them turning up at all, but I do wonder if they came just to see what the mysterious Freak House is like. Now that they've seen it and found it to be quite normal, I doubt they'll return again."

I suspected she was right, but didn't say so. "You didn't enjoy yourself at all? Not even a little bit?"

She thought for a moment. "Not particularly. I was too worried about everyone else enjoying themselves that I quite forgot about myself. I worried constantly about the new servants doing the right thing, and wishing Tommy were there to oversee it all. He's so competent, and everything runs smoothly when he's in charge. And of course that only led me to worry about his arm again and whether it would ever heal properly at all or...or not."

I squeezed her hand, but said nothing. She was clearly fond

of him, but whether it was enough to cope with what lay ahead if she acted upon her affections, I didn't know. To encourage her any more than I already had would be irresponsible.

* * *

I RETURNED to London the following day with Emily and Jacob. We were greeted at the door to their townhouse by the children, three of the senior members of staff, Samuel and Charity. The grave faces of the latter had us alarmed, but we listened to the children's stream of questions and long tales of what adventures they'd had in our absence before we retired to the sitting room.

"What is it?" Jacob asked as he waved off the footman who'd brought in the tea things.

"I can't find Alwyn." Samuel rubbed his jaw where a smattering of blond stubble had sprouted since we'd seen him the day before.

"Bloody hell." Jacob glanced at Emily and she cast a worried eye at the door.

"The children will be safe," Samuel assured her. "I've been up all night, searching for him, but didn't find him at his usual haunts and nobody has seen him. I collected Charity first thing this morning then came straight here."

"We asked the staff to be extra vigilant," Charity assured them. "So far, there's been no sign of trouble."

Emily sipped her tea and appeared perfectly calm, although I noticed her hand tremble.

"We must warn Jack and the others," I said. "Alwyn may not have returned to London at all."

"He did," Samuel said. "I asked at the Harborough station, and the stationmaster claimed a gentleman fitting Alwyn's description got on the train bound for London early yesterday morning. Alwyn is distinctive enough that I believe him."

Jacob drummed his thumb on his knee in an agitated rhythm. "Then we must remain alert until we find him."

Emily gave a firm nod. "I'm sure he'll show up."

"As am I," I said. "We have two more days anyway before he…before he said he will act."

"In the meantime, Charity must stay here," Emily declared. "Just until we know Alwyn has been found and hypnotized."

"Thank you," Charity and Samuel said at the same time.

We settled her into the guest bedroom next to mine, but instead of going to sleep there, she sat beside me in my bed. I was happy to have the company. Ever since Quin had left, I'd had trouble sleeping. I'd grown used to our nocturnal discussions and the comfort of simply knowing that he was close. Sleeping alone was so—well—lonely.

"How are the wedding plans?" I asked her.

"Coming together quickly, as a matter of fact." She sipped the hot chocolate that Emily had sent up earlier. I held my cup in my hands, warming them. "You'll receive an invitation soon."

"Is Mrs. Gladstone offering her assistance?" I knew Samuel's mother had initially been hesitant about her son marrying a woman with a sensational past, but she'd finally given their union her blessing.

"She's offered us every assistance. Of course, I've been sure to include her in the decisions along the way."

"All of them?"

She hid her grin behind the cup, but I caught the edge of its wickedness. "Oh yes. Every single one. I write to her every day and have even sent her sketches and fabric samples of my dress. I ask for her opinion, she sends it back, and then I do what I want."

I laughed. "That will only work so long as she remains at a distance."

"Thanks to Bert, she will. He doesn't need her there, of course, but she doesn't have to know that."

"That's kind of him."

"He said it was the least he could do after…after some of the problems he caused."

Problems that had now all gone away, thank goodness. I pecked her cheek. "I'm so happy for you. Both of you."

"Thank you. But what about you? You seemed out of sorts at the ball, even before Lord Alwyn spoke to you. Dare I ask, but is it Quin?"

I nodded. "I can't stop thinking about him."

Her lips flattened in sympathy. "Ordinarily I would encourage you to do everything you can to pursue happiness. After all, I'm living proof that obstacles can be overcome. But in your case, I hesitate to give that advice. I cannot see a way for you two to be together."

"I know. And please, don't worry about me. It *is* a hopeless situation, and I *will* be all right. I just need a little more time." I believed it. I truly did. At least, my head believed it. My heart hammered out a protest against my ribs that could not be easily ignored. "You must enjoy this time with Samuel."

She hugged me. "Thank you. I will. I am. But I don't want to ignore my friends after they've been so good to me."

I hugged her back. We stayed up talking into the night, mostly about Sylvia and Tommy, but also about the upcoming wedding and the Gladstone family.

The following day, after we returned from a walk in Hyde Park with the children, a letter was awaiting me.

"It's from Lord Alwyn," I announced to Emily and Charity.

They both stopped removing hats and gloves and stared at the letter. "What does it say?" Emily asked.

I read it while the nanny took the children upstairs and the butler gathered our things, then handed it to Emily. Charity watched her expectantly. I swallowed.

"'Call off your dog,'" Emily read. "'I don't know what Gladstone thinks he can do, but it won't work. You have twenty-four more hours in which to deliver the book to my house. I will know when you have done so. Remember what will happen if you do not.'" She folded it up and handed it back to me.

I held it with the tips of my finger and thumb as if it were poisonous, and took it up to my room. Later, Samuel and Jacob reported in. They'd been searching for Alwyn together all day. We did not need them to speak to know that they'd had no luck finding him. It was written all over their miserable faces.

"He seems one step ahead of us," Jacob said with a shake of his head. "Every time we hear he's at a certain club, we go there only to find he's just left."

"Surely he must sleep at some point," Charity said.

"It seems not."

"We lost him entirely before luncheon." Samuel scrubbed his hands through his messy hair and bowed his head. He looked exhausted.

Charity put her arm around him and brushed his hair back. "We'll find him. He can't hide forever."

But it felt like forever. Then the following afternoon, a little after the twenty-four hours was up, another letter arrived, hand delivered by an employee of Bethlem Hospital. It was addressed to Emily and Jacob. Emily gasped as she read, and Jacob's face grew grave. When they'd finished, they handed the letter to me. I read it through, feeling nothing as I did so. I didn't gasp or sigh or utter any words until I folded it up.

"It's my father," I told Charity and Samuel who'd been waiting patiently for us to finish. "He's dead."

CHAPTER 3

My father, François Moreau, had been committed to Bethlem Hospital shortly after I went to live in Melbourne with my brother, Louis, and his new wife, Celia. I had never felt much affection for him. My mother had deposited me with François when she knew she was dying, shortly before her death. He wasn't the ideal person to bring up a young girl, but there was nobody else. As far as she knew, I had no other family. My parents had never married and the circumstances of my birth were not imparted to me. I had never asked, having realized from a young age that there were some stories that didn't end well and should not be retold.

I ran my fingernail along the fold of the paper, sealing the contents as best as I could, much like I'd closed off the memories of my childhood. Some of them returned to me as I stood in the entrance hall of my niece's house. The bone-deep cold of a winter's night spent inside the one-room apartment I shared with François. The bigger neighborhood children pulling my hair as they called me names. The rest I managed to shut away before they brought on the sting of tears or the feeling of overwhelming hopelessness again.

François had not been cruel to me, but he had not taken on the role of father either. In fact, he largely ignored me. The only reason I had enough to eat was because I stole fruit or vegetables from his grocer's cart when I was hungry. His neglect may not have been a deliberate act but in my youth I hadn't really understood that he was mad. To me, many adults showed signs of madness. Drunks stumbled through the streets at all times of the day and the whores lifted their skirts for anyone with a coin. Many children were neglected until they were old enough to earn a few pennies, and husbands beat their wives until they fell unconscious. François's maniacal laughter and constant mutterings were just typical adult behavior, as far as I had been concerned.

Perhaps his madness was why I stopped laughing when he became my guardian. He seemed to do enough for the both of us. I stopped talking too, and it wasn't until Emily rescued me that I slowly returned to being myself. The time I spent with François became a blur, one that I preferred to forget. I'd done a good job of it too, since moving to Melbourne. Even returning to London had not brought the memories back. Only visiting François at Bethlem had. It was why I'd visited him only twice and had refused to go again.

Now, staring at the folded letter in my hand announcing his death, a part of me wished I'd had a chance to say one final goodbye. François's blood flowed through my veins. I was a medium because of him, and I was more resilient thanks to him. Perhaps I'd owed him at least a few words of acknowledgement.

"How did he die?" Charity's voice faltered as she looped her arm through mine. "Was it natural causes?"

"It doesn't say," Emily answered for me. She circled her

arm around my waist and squeezed. I hugged her back. François had been her grandfather and, although she'd never had much of a relationship with him, she must be feeling somewhat set adrift by the news too.

"We must find out," Jacob said. "We need to know if Alwyn got to him."

"You think he would dig into Cara's family tree to find him?" Samuel asked.

"It would have been easy enough, if one knows the right channels to investigate. If you think about it, François is the logical choice for Alwyn to target. He's Cara's nearest relation and he was kept in a minimum security wing at Bethlem. Alwyn could easily have found a way inside and ended François's life, perhaps making it look like the frail, elderly patient had died of natural causes."

"Oh God." I needed to sit down. Thankfully Emily and Charity steered me into the sitting room off the hall. Emily rang for refreshments while the others fussed over me, ensuring I was comfortable.

"It's not your fault," Charity told me. "Do you understand, Cara? You cannot blame yourself."

I nodded. I knew that, of course. And yet it sickened me to think that a simple fool like François could have been killed because of his link to me.

"That's if it was Alwyn," Jacob added. "I'll go to Bethlem and find out more. I need to make arrangements anyway. Gladstone, keep searching for Alwyn."

"I'll leave immediately."

"Emily, stay inside."

"Rest assured, we're not going anywhere," she said. "None of us."

The men departed just as tea was brought in. We ladies sat in silence, each of us lost to our own thoughts. Mine were not centered on the memories of my father, or on Alwyn himself, but on Quin and a single question I'd been asking myself over and over since I'd realized Alwyn might have killed François. Finally, I could stand it no longer. I had to ask the others for their opinion.

"Do you think this situation is important enough to summon Quin?"

The weighty silence was enough of an answer. Their sympathetic gazes only hammered it home. Emily set down her cup and took my hand in hers.

"Cara, this is not an otherworldly matter." Her gentle eyes searched mine. "In answer to your question, no I don't think it's important enough."

"Would he even be *allowed* to come?" Charity asked. "The administrators might forbid it if there was no reason for the summons."

"I know. You're right, of course." I let the matter rest there, unable and unwilling to give voice to my thoughts. They both knew anyway—I simply wanted to see Quin again.

The only logical thing we could do was wait. So we waited, something the three of us weren't particularly good at. We occupied ourselves with the children until Jacob's return later that day. He carried a box with him. Packed inside were my father's meager belongings. A comb, a clean white shirt, a brown cap, a book of hymns with a stiff spine, and a necklace made out of small bones.

"I'll send this to Louis," I said, inspecting the necklace. François had worn it under his shirt, hidden from view. "He ought to have it, since he was François's only son."

"The only one we know of," Emily said. At Jacob's shocked look, she shrugged. "He fathered Cara without anyone knowing, perhaps there were others."

"A sobering thought." I returned the necklace to the box. "I could have dozens of brothers and sisters."

"The girls would be mediums too," Charity said.

Emily and I had already discussed the possibility that the unknown third medium might be our relative, fathered or grandfathered by François. My brother Louis didn't know of any other children, but that didn't mean they didn't exist. He hadn't known about me, either, until I was ten years old.

I decided to write to him immediately, and sat down at Emily's escritoire in the small study adjacent to her private sitting room. It took some time before I found the right words to begin, only to be interrupted by Emily before I put pen to paper.

"Samuel's here!" She sounded breathless, as if she'd run up the stairs. "He has news."

"He's found Alwyn?"

"I don't know. The footman informed me of his arrival and I came straight here. I haven't seen him yet."

We raced downstairs together and found Samuel in the drawing room, talking quietly with Charity. Jacob joined us at the same moment, a footman having fetched him from his study. The faces of both Samuel and Charity told us nothing. Indeed, they were unusually blank. I wasn't sure what to make of it.

"You found him?" The urgency in Jacob's voice betrayed his worry.

Samuel quickly nodded and a collective sigh of relief filled the room. "Found him and hypnotized him."

Emily's hand fluttered to her chest as she blew out a breath. My knees felt a little weak and I sat on the nearest chair.

Jacob strode over to Samuel and slapped him on the back. "Good work. Where was he?"

"I found him at home, believe it or not. I'd paid a lad from Charity's school to keep watch there and report to my staff if Alwyn returned. Luckily I'd been coming home every two hours to check in or I would have missed him again. I had to hypnotize the Alwyns' butler into showing me to his master's bedroom. I woke Alwyn and hypnotized him while he was still trying to work out who I was. It was easy."

"What a relief," Emily said, collapsing on the sofa. "We ought to celebrate."

"Not quite." Samuel sagged against the window frame and folded his arms. He looked tired and haggard, an unusual state for the impeccably well-groomed gentleman. "After I hypnotized him I went to check on the book, just in case. It's gone."

"What?" The word exploded from all three of our mouths at once and had me shooting to my feet.

"Gone!" Jacob repeated. "How can it be gone? Didn't you hide it well enough?"

"Jacob, calm down," Emily warned.

Charity took Samuel's hand as he spoke. "I purchased a safe deposit box at a bank and left the book in it. Not my usual bank, and not Hatfield and Harrington, either. I used a false name," he added when Jacob opened his mouth to speak. Jacob shut it again with an audible snap of back teeth. "I wrote the details in a letter and had my lawyer place it with my other documents. His instructions were to leave it unopened unless one of us requested him to retrieve it."

"Somebody got to your lawyer," Jacob said darkly. He cursed under his breath.

I echoed it then asked, "Did you question him?"

Samuel nodded. "He claimed not to know what I was talking about. He said nobody asked him about it—as far as he can recall."

I cocked my head to the side. "You mean he can't recall everything?"

Samuel nodded again. "He claims to have lapses in his memory from yesterday."

"Bloody Myer," Jacob muttered. "He must have hypnotized him."

"I believe so too. He must have worked out that I was the logical choice for hiding the book from him. I was the only one who couldn't be hypnotized and forced into revealing the hiding place. Once he'd come to that conclusion, it wouldn't be too much of a stretch to question my lawyer under hypnosis, find my letter and open it."

"But he believed us when we told him Quin was the only one who knew where it was hidden," I said.

"Are you certain?"

"Ye-es. No. I don't know."

"Perhaps he believed Quin at first, but changed his mind later."

"Do you think he realized Quin wasn't from Melbourne after all?" Charity asked.

"How? Nathaniel assured me the night of the ball that he did not tell Myer his suspicions about Quin. He's as worried about Myer's obsession with the supernatural as we are and doesn't want him to possess the book either."

"You could ask him," Emily said with a smile that implied she hoped I would do more than merely ask.

"I would if I wanted to see him again. I'm not sure that I do."

"Why not? He's quite the dashing gentleman and his family are very nice, respectable people."

I twisted to face her fully. "You've been asking about him, haven't you? Emily! How could you?" Before she could answer, I added, "I am not interested in Nathaniel in that way anymore. I'm surprised you want me to be, since he's proven to be deceitful."

"That was in the past, and Myer may have forced his hand."

"You did not see his enthusiasm in the research library as

he hunted down clues of the book's whereabouts, nor see him sneak about the city as he followed us. Those are not the actions of a dashing gentleman, but a cowardly and untrustworthy one."

"Well," she huffed. "I didn't know you were so set against him now. You seemed to like him well enough at one point. You could speak of no one else after your voyage."

I turned my shoulder to her as she turned her shoulder to me.

Jacob cleared his throat and turned away from both of us. "Gladstone, we need to pay Myer a visit."

"I'm coming," I said before Samuel could respond. "I've had enough of sitting around here all day. I need to get out and do something."

Nobody forbade me and I departed in the coach with Samuel and Jacob immediately. It was growing late, the sun already setting behind the tall buildings, plunging the city into shadows. The shops had already shut for the evening and the streets were filled with speeding omnibuses overflowing with clerks and other office employees heading home to the outer suburbs.

We arrived at Myer's house and had to wait in the entrance hall while the butler informed his master. After his return, we were shown up to the study where Myer sat behind a desk that seemed much too large for the few pieces of paper and inkstand occupying it. I was pleased to be informed that Mrs. Myer was not at home. I had no interest in seeing her. She had a way of making me feel inferior, and that was without calling me names or staring like others did. She had a superior air about her, as if she were deigning to speak to you despite her better judgment. She even looked down on her husband.

Myer greeted us with smooth smiles and empty compliments. There was no sign of the anger he'd displayed the last time I'd seen him in Harborough, after being told the book was hidden. The change put me on edge. There had to be an explanation, and the only one I could think of was that he now possessed the book.

Jacob clearly thought the same way. He didn't exchange pleasantries with Myer. He leaned his knuckles on the desk and pinned Myer with an ice-cold glare. "Where is it?"

Myer held up his hands. "You'll have to be more specific, I'm afraid. I'm not a mind reader." He chuckled and his gaze flicked to Samuel.

Samuel rounded the desk and grasped the other man by the front of his waistcoat. "You know what Beaufort means. Where is the book?"

"Ah. That." Myer held up his hands in surrender and Samuel backed away. Myer smoothed down the front of his shirt and waistcoat. "I don't know. I believe your friend St. Clair hid it. Perhaps you ought to ask him. Oh, wait. Hasn't he sailed back to Melbourne?"

"Don't play games," Jacob snarled. "We know you hypnotized Gladstone's lawyer to get it."

"I don't know what you mean. Miss Moreau? Perhaps you can explain. Your temper is much more even than these two hot headed fellows. Hmmm?"

If only he knew I wanted to punch him in the nose. "We know you have it, Mr. Myer. We know how you got it. Hand it over now or you'll have to face their wrath. Unfortunately, I'm not able to control them, and I would hate to see you get hurt."

He swallowed heavily and took a moment to eye each of them in turn. He then rested his palms on the desk and spread out his fingers. "Gentlemen, please. Take a seat." Neither did. He swallowed again. "Perhaps you ought to cast your net a little wider than myself. For one thing, I know Lord Alwyn is after the book too."

"He doesn't have it," Samuel said.

"Are you certain?"

"Very. How did *you* know he wanted it?"

"He approached me with an offer. He said he knows that I want it and asked me what I'd be willing to pay if he found it."

"And your answer?"

"Was to tell him that he would have to travel all the way to the antipodes to learn of its location from the man who hid it. He responded to that with a scoff, if you must know. He was rather adamant that he could find it using other means. Don't ask me what they were. I refused to play his game."

"That may be so, but it wasn't him who took it."

Myer steepled his fingers and pressed them to his pursed lips as he thought. "But if St. Clair is the only one who knows where the book was hidden, and he has returned to Melbourne, how do you even know it's missing at all?" His eyes widened. "He wasn't the only one who knew, was he? Ha! You duped us all."

I was almost positive that he was acting, but I didn't dare accuse him. Samuel and Jacob were somewhat braver.

"Listen here," Jacob growled. "Stop pretending to be the fool. We know you're not. Alwyn doesn't have the book, so you must."

"Or not. What about Faraday?"

"What about him?" Samuel asked.

"He wanted the book as much as I did, and perhaps he suspected that St. Clair didn't hide it. Rather more interesting than that is the news of his disappearance."

"What do you mean?" I asked, taking a step closer to the desk.

"I can't find him." Myer looked more troubled by this than any threat from Jacob and Samuel. He frowned down at his hands. "He hasn't returned to his rented rooms in Chelsea for two days. I went in search of him this morning, and the landlady showed me about. All his things are still there, including his suitcase." He shook his head. "I can't figure it out. Where did he go in such a hurry?"

I exchanged glances with Samuel and Jacob. Their anger had dissolved quickly, this new mystery capturing their interest too. "Have you asked the police to look into it?"

"Or checked the hospitals?" Jacob asked.

"Yes to the police, no to the hospitals. They said they'd check for me if he doesn't turn up." Myer shook his head, his mouth set in a grim line. "But I suspect he doesn't want to be found. He's taken the book and gone into hiding. That's my theory."

I wasn't sure whether to believe him. Nathaniel did seem to have an interest in the book, but not as much as Myer. Besides, it didn't explain everything.

Samuel seemed to have the same thought as me. "Are you trying to tell me he can hypnotize too?"

"Not unless he's been hiding that particular light under a bushel. Why?"

"Because my lawyer experienced some memory lapses. Whoever took the book must have hypnotized him to get it. Do you have an explanation for that?"

Myer shrugged. "Old age, too much wine... Not all memory lapses are my fault, Gladstone. You know that."

A knock sounded on the door and Myer checked his watch as he called "Enter."

The butler bowed in the doorway. "Mrs. Myer has returned home, sir." His message delivered, he began to back out again before Myer asked him to halt.

"Adamson, show the gentlemen and Miss Moreau out. Excuse me," he said to us, "but I must ask you to leave now."

"We haven't finished," Jacob snapped.

"If you wish to stay I'm sure my wife will be delighted to have your company."

I snorted and everyone looked at me, including Adamson. I bit my lip and dipped my head.

"I have to go out," Myer went on. He strode past us to the door, but did not immediately walk through. Instead, he looked left then right, and only when he saw nobody out in the hall did he leave. It would seem he wanted to avoid his wife too.

We followed Adamson down the stairs to the front door, mercifully not bumping into Mrs. Myer either.

"What do you make of that?" I asked the others as the coach lurched forward. Twilight had descended upon the city while we were inside, and lamps were being lit by the lamplighter doing his rounds with his long pole. My stomach assured me it was dinnertime.

"It *must* have been Myer," Samuel said.

Jacob tapped his fingers on the window sill as he gazed out. "I'm not sure. He's right in that a lapse of memory could have other causes. And Faraday is missing."

"There is that. But Mr. Barry is neither old nor forgetful. I don't think his memory lapses can be explained away as easily as that. Myer must have hypnotized him."

"I tend to agree," I added. "Myer seemed to know all about the book and was a little too smug for my liking. But Nathaniel's disappearance is suspect. I wonder where he's gone and why so suddenly."

"Emily won't be happy," Jacob told me. When I looked at him askance, he added, "She hates it when her matchmaking plans go awry."

"I told her I'm not interested in Nathaniel."

"You showed a great deal of interest once. She hopes you will again when he disassociates himself from Myer."

I rolled my eyes and said nothing more. Arguing with

Jacob wouldn't get me anywhere. He was completely on Emily's side.

"Let's just find him first," Samuel said. "To be honest, I'm a little worried. Myer claimed Faraday took nothing with him from his rooms. That's something of a concern."

"Agreed." Jacob resumed his finger tapping. "I wonder where he went."

I wondered if he'd taken the book with him.

* * *

My father was buried on a cool, wet day that seemed out of place for June. The rain came down in a fine drizzle as we watched his coffin descend into the ground, but stopped as the coach rolled away from the cemetery. By the time we reached the Belgravia house, the sun was out, or as out as it could ever be in London's haze.

It had been four days since we'd spoken to Myer, and Nathaniel still had not turned up. Nor were we any closer to finding the book. Samuel even went so far as to hypnotize members of Myer's household, but none knew anything about a book of spells or the disappearance of Nathaniel Faraday. It was an unsettling time but, as each day passed and nothing happened, we began to relax. The household resumed its routine as if it had never been interrupted. Charity returned to the school and her teaching duties, while I became listless with boredom. The universities didn't run lectures during summer and there was little to do in a city heating up by the day. Unfortunately that meant I had no excuses when invited out to drink tea or dine with Emily and her friends. Some I enjoyed, like the musical evenings hosted by Jacob's mother, Lady Preston, or Adelaide Culvert, but others were tedious affairs. I was quite sure I nodded off during one afternoon of poetry reading. In my defense, it was a warm day and the reader was a gentleman poet in love with the hostess's daughter. He possessed bucked teeth and a lackluster imagination, ending every verse with a reference to the girl's 'fine eyes'.

I was quite glad when Emily announced we would be spending the rest of the summer at Lord and Lady Preston's estate in the country. I loved Jacob's family's rambling house, set in acres of parkland and wood. There was so much to do there, and so many places to explore. Even better, there were few neighbors nearby. The invitations to afternoon tea and dinners would be fewer.

The night before we left, however, my plans changed. A telegram arrived from Jack Langley, begging either Emily or myself to travel quickly to Frakingham. The telegram didn't specify why, but it must have been a ghostly problem for him to ask only for us.

Emily agreed that I could go without her, since she wanted to be with the children. I caught the first train out of London and arrived in Harborough in the afternoon. My telegram had been received and the Langley coach was waiting for me, along with Jack and Hannah.

"Thank God you're here!" Hannah threw her arms around me in a more exuberant embrace than I'd ever received from her.

I arched my brows over her shoulder at Jack. He gave me a grim smile. "I'm sorry, Cara, but we'll have to travel onto the house later. This ghostly problem needs immediate attention." He picked up my valise and strode off to the coach.

Hannah grabbed my hand and dragged me along in her wake. I trotted to keep up, my free hand clamped down on my hat to stop it falling off in the rush.

"Is the ghost a violent one?" I asked as we climbed into the cabin.

Jack gave the driver instructions then shut the door. "Violent, mad, or simply mischievous, it's difficult to tell. It throws things around, smashes windows, plates, whatever it can get its hands on."

"Constantly?"

"No. Just every now and again. As soon as we think all is quiet and it has left this realm, it'll toss something about. It's almost as if it wants to remind us that it's still there."

"At least it's not too destructive."

"Tell that to the building's owner," Jack muttered.

"But that's not the greatest concern." Hannah blinked her dark blue eyes at me. "The problem isn't so much the ghost creating a disturbance, although that is troubling enough. It's that it can move about freely."

I narrowed my gaze. "That's impossible."

"Are you sure? Because this one can come and go from the building at will. It has even been up to Frakingham House and around the ruins. There have also been reports of disturbances here in the village."

I blanched. "That is very unusual. Are you sure there isn't more than one spirit?"

They exchanged a glance. "There could be, but you've never noticed a spirit at Freak House before."

"True."

"And nobody has died there recently. Aside from Lord Malborough, that is."

"He died down at the ruins," I reminded her. "If he decided to haunt this realm, he would be confined there."

"Perhaps he's the one who moved the stones at the ruins then," Jack said more to Hannah than to me.

Hannah nodded. "It's possible. I'm afraid you may be quite busy, Cara, if there is more than one ghost. It would seem Harborough is infested with them."

"Then it's fortunate that we're starting immediately."

We left the village and drove down a country lane so narrow that two coaches would have had difficulty passing one another. A wooded forest stretched along the left hand side of the road, and a low hedge of hawthorn lined the right. Shards of sunlight pierced the forest canopy, spotlighting a small bush here, a fallen trunk there. It was a pretty but remote scene.

I was about to ask how far we had to travel when the endless line of the hedge was finally broken to accommodate a rusty gate. Beyond it was a garden that may have once been pretty and neat but was now overrun with knotty brambles, wild roses and weeds. But it was the house being devoured by ivy that caught my attention. It was a large red brick Tudor building with a steeply pitched roofline and several chimney pots shooting into the blue sky. The windows were small, the panes either broken or missing altogether, and one boarded up entirely. Some of the roof tiles were in a similar state and I hated to think what the weather had done to the inside.

"It's been abandoned for twenty years," Jack said, opening the coach door for me.

Jack ordered Hannah to stay back with the footman and driver, but she merely snorted in answer and followed us. The first prickle of apprehension slithered down my spine at the sound of a surly male voice coming from inside the building.

"Someone's here!" he shouted.

I glanced at Jack and Hannah. "Did either of you hear that?" I whispered.

They shook their heads. So my ghost was inside. I blew out a breath and reached for the doorknob.

The door swung open before I touched it and a blur of white flew at me. Jack's hand whizzed past my face, knocking the object against the wall where it shattered. The pieces clattered onto the stoop where they disintegrated into even smaller shards on the stone. It had been a dinner plate.

"Bloody hell!" I cried, hands on hips. If there's one thing I've learned from being a medium, it's to show the spirits that you're not afraid of them. Sometimes they only wanted to instill fear. Many had not, after all, been particularly nice people when they'd been alive, and their characters hadn't improved much upon their deaths. If I were to convince them to cross over, I needed to gain their respect. "What did you do—?"

I stopped. Stared. The spirit of a giant red-bearded fellow glared back at me, his pose just as defiant as the one I was attempting. I lowered my hands to my sides, no longer feeling brave, or defiant, or anything except confused. There wasn't one spirit staring back at me.

There were dozens.

They perched on the thick, black ceiling beams that spanned the width of the room, swinging their legs in the air. They sat on filthy mattresses on the floor, idly rubbing the broken skin at their throats. They stood on the central table, stuffing entrails back into their bodies. They were mostly men, all adults, and wore different styles of clothing that covered centuries of fashion. They stared back at me with dead eyes.

Then the red-bearded one grinned, revealing stumps of rotting teeth. "Ye can see us, can't ye, lass?"

One of the spirits jumped down from the beam and landed awkwardly on his knees. The leap would have broken a living man's bones, but he got up and snapped his crooked leg into place.

"Pretty girl, you are." He licked bruised and cut lips. "Come for some fun, eh?"

"She alive or dead?" asked another man with pock marks on his face, neck and hands.

"And what about them? They dead too?"

"Let's see, eh?" said Redbeard. He picked up a sword that I hadn't noticed on the table beside him, bared what was left of his teeth, and ran at me.

Jack pulled me behind him and slammed the door shut. The sound of splintering wood had us jumping back and my heart leaping into my throat.

"Go!" Jack shouted, grabbing our hands and pulling us down the steps. We streamed through the garden and I lost my hat to an overhanging branch covered in thorns. We reached the coach just as a knife flew past my head.

I scrambled into the cabin and Jack shoved Hannah in after me in a most unladylike manner that sent her sprawling on the seat opposite.

"Drive on!" he called out as he jumped inside. He helped Hannah to sit up as the coach sped away.

I hazarded another look out the window and saw Redbeard and three others standing at the gate, doubled over with laughter as if they'd never seen anything so amusing. The hedge soon obscured them from view.

I blew out a breath and regarded my companions gravely. "We have a very big problem."

"Perhaps mischievous isn't the right word to describe that spirit," Hannah said grimly.

"No. Nor is spirit."

"Pardon?"

Jack leaned forward, his intense gaze on mine. "What do you mean?"

"I mean there isn't one spirit, there are many. Perhaps thirty or more."

"Bloody hell. Where did they all come from?"

"And why are they here now?" Hannah chimed in.

"I can't do this on my own," I told them.

"Agreed." Jack went to pull down the window to speak to

the driver. Fresh country air blasted my face and teased the hair that had come loose from its knot during our flight. I regretted the loss of my perky little black hat with the half veil. "We'll return to the village and send a telegram to Emily."

"No. Shut the window, please, Jack."

He did as I asked and sat back to wait for me to elaborate.

"We're not going to contact Emily. There are too many, even with two of us, and they're too dangerous. Besides, I suspect they won't be easily convinced to cross over. They're having too much fun."

"Then what do you suggest?" Hannah asked.

"We need to summon Quin."

CHAPTER 4

"Are you sure this is a good idea?" Sylvia hadn't stopped frowning at me since we informed her that Quin would be summoned. However, she had dutifully retrieved the parchment upon which the spell to summon him was written and brought it to us in the sitting room.

"Of course it's a good idea," I said. "We discussed it on the drive from the village and it was decided. Now, may I have the parchment, please?" I held out my hand, but she didn't place the wooden tube containing the rolled up page on my palm.

"Actually, *you* decided," Jack said. "I think it requires further deliberation."

I curled my fingers and pulled back my fist. "Why?"

"We know so little about this fellow."

"I know a great deal about him, as it happens. I understand your hesitation, Jack. You haven't met Quin. I assure you he's a gentleman in every sense of the word."

"He's a knight," Sylvia said, as if that made a difference.

Hannah looked impressed. "A knight. How intriguing."

Jack scowled at his wife. "Why?"

"I've never met a genuine medieval knight."

He *humphed*. "Isn't he dead?"

"In a way," I said, somewhat vaguely. If they knew Quin was from Purgatory, they'd think again about summoning him. "He's been assigned warrior duties and comes to this realm, and perhaps others, when summoned. He's only summoned when necessary." I held out my hand again to Sylvia. "I think a tribe of dangerous spirits is a valid reason to summon him."

"Can he send them back?" Jack asked.

I had no idea. He was more than capable of battling demons, but he couldn't see ghosts and certainly couldn't communicate with them. What, in fact, could he do?

I dismissed my own question. Surely he could do *something* to help. We would find out when he arrived. "We really shouldn't waste any more time. Sylvia, tell Jack and Hannah that Quin was no trouble at all."

"It's true," she said as she pulled out the aged parchment from the tube. "He's a good fellow and proved very useful. You should have seen him fight off the demons! He's better than even you, Jack, and you're quite good."

"Thank you," he said wryly.

Hannah smothered a smile.

"The spell, if you please, Sylvia." I held out my hand once more. This time she placed the parchment on it, but did not let go.

"You seem to be mistaken about my warning," she said, lowering her voice. "I wasn't asking whether summoning him was a good idea for us and the situation we find ourselves in. I was asking if it were a good idea for *you*."

I swallowed and tightened my grip on the parchment in case she decided to withdraw it. "Thank you for your concern, but I'll be all right."

I didn't look to Hannah and Jack, but I had the distinct

feeling they were glancing at one another. I tugged on the parchment roll and Sylvia released it. The words to summon Quin were out of my mouth before anyone could question my motives further.

A whisper of air swept through the sitting room, rustling the pages of Sylvia's fashion journal. I held my breath, suddenly afraid that he wouldn't come, or that he'd be angry that I summoned him for this.

Then he was there, in all his semi-naked glory, his arms crossed over his massive chest, his sword strapped to his hip. His dark hair fell raggedly over his forehead, stopping just above his eyes. His direct, uncompromising gaze settled on me, making my blood throb and my head giddy. I breathed. Breathed again.

He was here.

I smiled and was immeasurably relieved to receive a crooked one in return. "Good afternoon, Quin. Welcome back."

"Cara." My name rumbled from the depths of that impressive chest and rolled off his tongue. He crossed the room with a few long strides and knelt on one knee before me. That all-seeing gaze searched my face. "Are you unwell again?"

Jack, who'd shot to his feet the moment Quin arrived, came to stand beside me. Quin's nostrils flared, but he otherwise gave no indication that he was aware of Jack's presence.

"I'm well," I said. "Your wounds seem to have healed." The scratches and claw marks from the demons were visible as faint scars on his chest and shoulders, but there were none on his face.

"Earthly wounds heal faster in my realm. So if you're not ill...?"

"We summoned you for another purpose."

I was about to tell him our problem, when Jack thrust out his hand. "Jack Langley. This is my wife, Hannah."

Quin stood and shook Jack's hand then bowed to Hannah and Sylvia. "You are a relation to Miss Langley's?" he asked Jack.

"Her cousin, and nephew of August Langley. Hannah and I were on our honeymoon when you were last here."

"How long ago was that?"

"A few weeks," I told him, rising. "You really don't notice the passage of time, do you?"

One corner of his mouth kicked up. "No. If I did, I would have gone mad by now."

"Where is it you're from?" Jack asked.

"Another realm." Quin managed to hide his frustration at the question rather well, but I heard the edge to his response. "Something has happened here for you to summon me. Are there demons?"

"Only Jack," Sylvia said with a nervous little laugh. "He's half-demon."

"Sylvia," Hannah hissed.

"I already know what he is," Quin assured her.

"How?" Jack asked.

"I just do."

Jack looked as if he would ask another question, so I quickly said the first thing that came to mind. "How have you been?" *Ugh.* I sounded like an idiot.

"I am as I've always been."

"I see." I think he meant he hadn't been punished in any way. Although the administrators in Purgatory had allowed him to help me while I was ill, they'd not known he also wanted the book for his own purposes. Not then. I wasn't yet certain if they'd found out. I suspected they saw everything here and in other realms, but I couldn't be sure.

"You need some clothes," Sylvia said. "I think we have

your suit from the last time somewhere. Mrs. Moore ought to know where it is."

"And someone needs to inform August," Jack said. "Sylvia, would you mind?"

"Why not you?"

He arched his eyebrows at her and jerked his head at Quin. Clearly he thought he needed to stay and chaperone. I refrained from telling him that I'd been alone with Quin on countless occasions last time, and I would be again. There were so many things I wanted to say to him, but mostly I just wanted to be near him. If I had to sneak into his bedroom at night, I would.

Sylvia left, huffing and shaking her head in frustration. Once upon a time she would have done as her cousin asked dutifully. Now, she seemed more inclined to want to be part of the action. I couldn't blame her.

"How is Dawson?" Quin asked me.

"Tommy's doing as well as can be expected," I said. "It will be some time before he heals entirely, if at all, but there's been no infection and he's up and about."

"I'm pleased. I would like to see him again, and the silent one."

"Bollard is with Mr. Langley now. I'm sure they'll be happy to see you again too."

"There's little time for chit chat," Jack said. "We'll head back to the house immediately."

"What house?" Quin asked.

At the same moment I said, "Not tonight."

Jack chose to answer Quin first. "We have a problem with ghosts at a house on the outskirts of the village, as well as other spots nearby, including at the abbey. Is that something you can help us with?"

Quin's gaze slid to me. "There are too many for you, Cara?"

I nodded. "Too many and they're rather dangerous. One nearly sliced my head off with a dinner plate. I don't think they want to leave."

"Then you were right to call me. I can help." He glanced out the window where dusk was casting its veil over the countryside. "We'll begin in the morning."

"Why not now?" Jack asked.

"I can do many things, but seeing in the dark is not one of my talents."

"Modest fellow," Jack muttered under his breath.

"We'll begin in the morning," Quin repeated.

"We?" Jack echoed.

"Cara must be with me. I need her powers as a medium. I can't see spirits, but I can fight them."

"Can you send them back to the waiting area?"

"No."

"What about speak to them and convince them to cross over?"

"I'm a fighter."

"*I* can bloody fight them!" Jack snapped.

Hannah looped her hand through her husband's arm. "Yes, but Mr. St. Clair is an otherworldly warrior. He can't be harmed as you can."

I lowered my gaze, not prepared to tell her that Quin was susceptible to the same dangers as any mortal on Earth. He was harder to injure, but he could still die or succumb to illness. It was only when he was in his own realm that he was immortal.

"What will fighting them do if you can't return them to the waiting area?" Jack said.

"They won't be returned," Quin said. "Their souls will be destroyed. They'll cease to exist."

Hannah gasped. I pressed my hand to my chest where my

heart had been beating erratically ever since Quin's arrival. "That sounds very…final," she said.

"It is. You'll need to warn them first, Cara, and give them a chance to return to the waiting area. If they still choose to remain and cause harm to the living, I will act. You can only help, Langley, if you have an otherworldly blade."

"I do," Jack said with a note of defiance. "It's a knife forged in the demon realm. We won't need your sword then."

"My blade is longer than yours."

"I thought only otherworldly creatures could destroy a spirit's soul," I said quickly, interrupting their power-struggle. "That's what Emily told me."

Quin shook his head. "It's the otherworldly blade that destroys. It doesn't matter who holds it."

It was rather a lot to take in, and the thought of taking away someone's afterlife chilled me.

"What hour is it?" Quin asked, picking up the clock on the mantel and turning it on its side.

I plucked it out of his hands and returned it to mantel. "You must learn to tell the time on this visit. Why do you need to know the hour?"

"I want to know if I've missed dinner."

I laughed. "There's another two hours before we dine. Are you hungry?"

"I can wait."

His response brought out the hostess in Hannah. "Would you like an appetizer?"

"An appetizer would be very nice, Mrs. Langley. Thank you."

She tugged on the bell pull while Quin turned slowly to observe the room. I could see him noting the subtle changes that Hannah had already introduced, mostly in the uncluttering of the table surfaces.

He had hardly turned much at all when I leapt off the

chair with a gasp. "Quin!" I stared wide-eyed at his bare back. The two long scars still crisscrossed the broad expanse, but now there were more. Many more. They sliced horizontally between his shoulder blades all the way down to the band of his leather pants. Unlike the old white ones, these were red, raw, the flesh raised into ridges. "What happened?"

He spun around, obscuring his back from my view. "It's nothing for you to concern yourself with."

"But I am concerned." I gripped his arm near his shoulder and tried to turn him around again, but he wouldn't budge.

He folded his arms and scowled at me.

"What is it?" Hannah asked. "Is something wrong with his back?"

"He just has one or two more scars than last time." I couldn't ask him more questions while others were present. Quin's answers—if he deigned to supply any—might give away too much about the realm he'd traveled from, and I didn't want them to know he was from Purgatory.

I let him go and sat down again, feeling a little sick. The footman arrived a moment later, and too late I realized we hadn't informed the servants of our guest's arrival. The new ones had not been present during Quin's last visit, so it was easy enough to explain that he'd arrived on foot and we'd spotted him through the window and let him in through the garden entrance. Of course, he'd lost his luggage and had his suit stolen. Whether the footman believed the fanciful story wasn't clear from his shocked stare. He left with orders to bring some cheese and fruit. No doubt he would delight in gossiping about Quin belowstairs.

"Perhaps we should have waited for the shirt to arrive," Hannah said.

Jack sighed. "We'll have a devil of a time convincing them to believe that story, Cara. Did it work last time?"

"Yes, but there were fewer servants last time and all of

them were used to strange goings on at the house. We'll need to tell them that Quin didn't leave England after all, to account for his reappearance after such a short absence."

Sylvia returned with clothes, Tommy, and her uncle, wheeled by Bollard. The three men clasped Quin's hand in greeting and seemed pleased to have him back. Their obvious enthusiasm must have eased Jack's mind. He sat for the first time since Quin's arrival.

Quin didn't leave the room to put on the shirt and waistcoat, but threw them on where he stood. He left off the tie, much to Sylvia's displeasure. The ensemble looked out of place on him and he looked uncomfortable wearing it. He would hate donning a jacket at dinnertime.

"You need to go down to the ruins first and remove Malborough's ghost," Langley said after we explained why we'd summoned Quin. "He's disturbing the stones, and the gardener is beginning to grow suspicious."

"We told him it must be village children, come to poke about on a dare," Hannah said. "But I think he's been watching carefully and hasn't seen anyone, and yet the stones still move."

"We can do that this evening." I looked to Quin. "If it's only the one spirit, we ought to be safe enough. It's meeting the pack of them in the Tudor house that has me worried."

"Tonight," Quin said without moving his heavy-lidded gaze from me. "As you wish."

I swallowed and looked away. The promise in his voice spoke of more than mere ghost hunting. "We'll go as soon as you've eaten something."

The footman arrived with the fruit and cheese, and Quin wolfed the selection down in a few moments. Either he was starving or he wanted to get to work quickly.

"I'll come with you," Jack said as we rose to leave.

"No!" I cleared my throat and thanked my ancestors for a

skin color that didn't show blushes. "It's quite all right. Thank you, Jack."

Hannah rested her hand on his arm. It looked innocuous enough, but when her knuckles went white and his eyes widened at her, I realized she was squeezing rather hard. Her glare connected with his, and finally he seemed to understand what she was silently telling him. He glanced at me then at Quin and gave a resigned shrug. He must have been glad he wasn't my guardian.

I shrugged on my jacket and gloves for the stroll down to the ruins. It may have been summer, but the air had cooled considerably after the sun went down. At least there was no mist, and the circle of light cast by my lamp kept the darkness at bay. I made sure we were out of earshot of the house before I spoke.

"How did you get those scars?"

"I wondered how long it would be before you asked." He smiled at me. Smiled!

"Quin, this isn't funny. Your back is covered."

"Is it? I can't see."

"Stop avoiding the question and tell me. Was it the administrators?"

"They are the ones who mete out punishment."

I stopped and grabbed his arm. "You were punished? For coming to me?"

"Not precisely. I was allowed to help you, but not allowed to seek the book for my own reasons, and especially not to use it to leave Purgatory."

"How do they know that was your motive for coming?"

His lip curled into a sneer. "They know everything."

I took his hand in my own and his strong step faltered and slowed. "So they whipped you."

He gave a single nod. "It's only flesh, Cara. I have no need of it anymore."

No, I suppose he didn't. He had no need of any earthly things. "Quin, I'm sorry—"

He stopped abruptly and rounded on me. His fingers dug into my shoulders. "Don't. Don't apologize for not giving me the book. It was the right thing to do." He let me go. "It would have been far worse for me if I had succeeded in gaining the book but failed to escape."

And if he hadn't failed? What then?

He could not have come back to me here, now. He would have gone on to his afterlife, unable to return to this realm.

There were so many things I wanted to ask him and tell him, but I knew from past experience that he would only grow angry with the questions and not answer anyway. Besides, it seemed strange to admit that I'd been researching him in history books.

Instead, he asked me questions about my family's health and what I'd been doing in the last few weeks. I was about to tell him that the book had gone missing, but thought better of it. I couldn't be certain what sort of reaction I'd receive, and we had arrived at the ruins anyway.

"Can you see anyone?" he asked.

I held up the lamp, but its weak light didn't reach beyond three feet in any direction. "It seems quiet. Lord Malborough!" I called. "Are you here? If so, please reveal yourself. I'm a medium and wish to speak to you."

Silence.

"I know the circumstances under which we last met weren't ideal."

Quin grunted out a soft laugh.

"But I do hope we can look past that and discuss your future."

"I don't have a future!" came a voice from the shadows. "Leave me be."

"I can't. You're upsetting the...ladies." I almost said

servants, but a snob like Malborough wouldn't care about the staff.

"You think I give a damn about women?"

It would seem I'd overestimated his chivalrous streak. "What am I to do to convince him?" I whispered to Quin. "He won't even come closer."

"Leave it to me." He withdrew his sword.

"You're going to destroy him now without even a warning?"

"I don't plan on using it on him. Yet." He held the sword at arm's length, point down. "Malborough! I'll let you have one swing at me."

"Quin! What are you doing? He'll hurt you, perhaps even kill you."

"Will he?" His idle words matched his smile.

"You told me so yourself. You're mortal here. Even if he doesn't kill you, a wound could turn septic. Unless the rules have changed since you were last here?"

"The rules never change."

"Then give me the sword." I went to snatch it from his hand, but he moved it out of my reach. I leapt at it again, and he moved it again, catching me as I stumbled. His firm grip across my middle felt warm, familiar.

I touched his hand and glanced up at him, only to see him staring back as if he were surprised at what he'd caught. Then his gaze turned smoky and his thumb inched up to my ribs and rubbed through my clothes.

"Very well," interrupted a limp voice.

I turned to see the doughy form of Malborough waxing and waning in the low light. I gagged and covered my mouth with my hand. He was a gruesome sight, thanks to the demon attack that had ended his life. The flesh hung off his body in long, pulpy strips, and he was missing both ears, a hand, and a chunk of his scalp. I imagined other bits had come off him too, but his bloodied clothing covered the rest of him. Bile burned my throat and I had to swallow heavily to force it down.

"He's here," I told Quin.

He let me go and held out the sword again. "My lord?" He bowed, lowering his gaze.

"What trick is this?" Malborough asked.

"No trick," I said. "He will allow you one lunge with his blade."

"What's the point? He'll step out of the way."

"It may make you feel better. I know you harbor some ill will against him, considering the role he played in your death."

He turned cold, fathomless eyes on me. "I suppose you're going to tell me it's my fault."

"You did summon the demons that killed you."

He gave a humorless laugh. "And you think taking one swipe at your warrior will soothe my anger enough that I'll leave?"

"It's worth a try. If there's anyone else you'd like me to fetch here for you to speak to then please tell me. Your father, perhaps?"

"I've already been to see him. Fool. He was terrified out of his wits. Had no clue it was me come to haunt him."

"Oh? Has your father been here?"

"No."

"Then how did you haunt him?"

"I went to his London home. You are a silly twit, aren't you?"

I held up my hand, slowing him down. Quin edged closer to me as if he sensed something was wrong. "But you died here, and spirits can't leave the place where they died."

He shrugged. "I feel a stronger connection to these ruins, it's true. But I've been all over the place since I was called back. Here, London, my house." He nodded at the manor.

"That's impossible."

"What's he saying, Cara?" Quin asked.

"That he is not confined to a single place since his death."

"No," Malborough said with a huff of impatience. "You're not listening, stupid girl. Not since my death. Since my *return*. After my death, I haunted the ruins for a day or so and realized there was no point. So I went to the waiting area and crossed over, when they finally decided where I should go." He wiped his mouth on his sleeve and looked nervously about. "But I was called back here recently."

I relayed what he'd said to Quin, then added, "Spirits can't come back from their final resting place. Once they've crossed, they've crossed."

"Clearly you know nothing about the afterlife," Malborough said. "Because I'm not the only one who came back."

"How many others?"

"Dozens." He shrugged. "We didn't perform a roll call."

"Was one of them a big fellow with a red beard and Scottish accent?"

He nodded. "Bloodthirsty barbarian, that one. Glad I didn't have to stay with him and his lot."

I shook my head, over and over. It didn't make sense. Spirits who could wander about was one thing, but dangerous spirits was quite another, particularly if they didn't want to return to…where? "Malborough, you said you crossed. Did you go to, uh, that dark place?"

"Hell?" His laugh held the high pitch of madness and the cold steel of cruelty. "You could call it that."

I glanced at Quin and nodded gravely.

"When did this happen?" Quin asked.

"Time has little meaning for me," Malborough said. "Perhaps a day or more."

I repeated his answer for Quin's benefit then turned back to Malborough. "You have to return," I said. "You don't belong here."

"You want me to go back to hell? Willingly?" He snorted.

"Lord Malborough, please. Be reasonable. The good people here are frightened."

"They have every right to be. And they are not good people." In a blur of motion, he snatched the sword from Quin and sliced it through the air so fast, I had no time to scream let alone dive out of the way. I could only put up my hands as the blade plunged toward me.

CHAPTER 5

Malborough was fast, but Quin was faster. He shoved my shoulder and I tumbled out of the way, landing on my side on the soft earth. I managed to hang onto the lantern and mercifully it remained lit. The sword glinted in the light as Quin dodged its blade in a move far smoother than the one I'd just executed.

I opened my mouth to warn Quin that he couldn't fight a ghost, but shut it again. He knew his fists would sail right through Malborough, and my talking would only distract him. Ordinarily, Quin could easily trip Malborough or grab his wrist, but none of those techniques would work on a spirit. All Quin could do was keep out of the blade's way until Malborough dropped it.

Or so I thought. With only one hand, Malborough couldn't raise the massive sword very high, but he could use it like a lance, and he charged straight at Quin. Quin didn't move.

I screamed and watched helplessly as the sword bore down on him. At the last possible moment, he swerved to his left. The blade missed him, but the ghostly form passed through his body. Malborough's momentum propelled him forward. It was then that I realized Quin had positioned himself in front of one of the ruined walls. Malborough slammed into it with a grind of metal on stone as the sword hit the wall with him.

The collision with a solid, inanimate object wouldn't harm a ghost, but it did slow him down. While Malborough staggered to his feet, Quin wrenched the sword out of his hands.

"Blast!" Malborough cowered against the wall, his terrified gaze on the sword as it plunged toward him. He could have moved either left or right and not been seen by Quin, but he didn't. He was rooted to the spot.

"Wait!" I shouted. "We must inform him of his options."

But Quin didn't wait. Even in the semi-darkness the fierce gleam in his eyes was unmistakable. They held no mercy, no forgiveness, only fury. He thrust the sword into Malborough's chest, opening up a gaping black hole. The ghost's mouth opened in a soundless scream. His wide eyes watched Quin reach inside and pull out a dark, pulsing mass.

"What's that?" Malborough asked, his voice quavering.

"Your soul," I whispered.

Quin squeezed and the mass turned to dust. It filtered through his fingers onto the grass, forming a small pile. The spirit of Malborough followed, his final words garbled as he disintegrated.

I stared at the dust. My hands shook, rattling the lantern cage. I set it on the ground and pressed my hands together in front of me.

The sound of Quin sheathing his sword turned me in his direction. He blinked slowly at me, not at the remains of Malborough, and seemed unsure of what to do next. I felt the same way. What he'd just done was quite possibly the worst thing that could ever happen to a being. To be extinguished entirely, never to exist in any plane ever again...it was unfathomable.

He held out his hand to me. "Are you all right, Cara?"

I stared at his hand until he retracted it. "Yes."

"He didn't deserve an afterlife."

I picked up the lantern and got to my feet. Quin took my elbow to assist me. "Not even in hell?"

"No. You're dismayed at what I did." It wasn't a question.

"Shocked is perhaps a more appropriate term. You didn't give me a chance to warn him. He might have chosen to return to hell, rather than become nothing."

"They never choose to return, and there was no time to explain. I had to strike before he moved or I would be at a disadvantage."

"Yes, but..." Perhaps Quin was right, but it still made me feel as though we'd murdered someone. Malborough wasn't a good man, but did he deserve nothingness? Did anyone?

Quin touched my cheek, sweeping back a curl that had come loose and tucking it behind my ear. The gentle gesture got my full attention, and our gazes locked. "This is what I do, Cara. I remove the black, rotten souls of otherworldly creatures, including spirits."

"It's just so...final. I would have liked to have warned him, given him a choice."

He dropped his hand to his side. A muscle pulsed in the unforgiving planes of his jaw. "I've told you before, I'm not always a good person. I have a temper and I sometimes act on it. He was a threat to us both, and I did what I had to do to remove the threat."

I sighed. "I know. Come on, let's go and tell the others then dress for dinner."

We walked back to the house in silence. My thoughts

were troubled, but I couldn't feel sorry for Malborough. He'd hurt too many people in his life, and perhaps nothingness was better than an afterlife in the dark place where cruel souls were sent.

We told the others that Malborough was gone; body, spirit and soul. They didn't seem upset that Malborough had been destroyed.

We dispersed to dress and reconvened in the dining room some time later. I wore an off the shoulder gown the color of a heady red wine. It caught Quin's attention. I could feel his warm gaze touching my bare skin—until the food arrived. He tucked into the fish course and finished before most of us were half way through. He was about to wipe his mouth with the back of his sleeve until he recalled where—and when—he was and used the napkin. At least he'd remembered to use both knife and fork.

"Did Malborough tell you why he came back to haunt us?" Langley asked, after dismissing the servants. "Did he want to punish us? Was he very mad?"

"It's a curious situation," I said, frowning at my plate. I set down my cutlery, no longer hungry. "He had already crossed over, but had an opportunity to return."

"Isn't that impossible? I admit to knowing little about spirits, and the laws that bind them, but I thought once they crossed they were gone."

"It's what I've always thought too," I told him. "But Malborough proved otherwise. He claimed to have come back."

"From where?" Hannah asked. "Beyond the waiting area?"

I nodded. "The place he'd been sent to wasn't somewhere he wanted to return."

Sylvia gave a little whimper and also set down her knife and fork.

"Is he connected to the other spirits at the Tudor house?" Jack asked.

I nodded. "It seems several spirits have returned after crossing over. The usual rules of haunting don't apply to them, and they can travel where they like and haunt anywhere. Malborough has already been to London, but chose to return here to Frakingham."

"Why not the Tudor house?"

"He didn't like the company."

Hannah now set down her cutlery and pushed her plate away. "That implies that the ghosts at the Tudor house are even more dangerous than he was."

"Hence the plate-throwing," Jack muttered.

"They're from the same place that Malborough was sent by the administrators."

"It's called Hell, Cara." Sylvia took up her knife and fork again and stabbed her fish. "You can say the word. I won't suffer from the vapors if I hear it."

"Hell is just one name for it," Quin told her. "It goes by many names."

"Have you been there?" Jack asked.

Hannah gasped. "You can't ask that."

He shrugged. "Why not? It's a perfectly good question. He does seem to have traveled extensively."

"No," Quin said. His lips didn't curve up, but I could swear he found Jack's question amusing. "I've not been to Hell."

How different was Hell to Purgatory? Going by the scars on Quin's back, I would say not very much.

"I wonder if this is only happening at Harborough," I said in an attempt to steer the conversation to safer territory. "If spirits are manifesting all over the place, we're going to have quite a task to round them all up and send them back."

"We haven't heard of any disturbances elsewhere," Jack said. "Not even from the other villages."

"And there was nothing reported in London before I left. Not that I am aware, anyway."

"That implies the portal has something to do with it," Langley said.

"Aye." Quin nodded slowly, his attention focused on the door as if he expected spirits to wander in. "They must have come through it together."

"How? Why?"

"It must have been opened—"

"Opened!" Sylvia cried, once more abandoning her food. "Who would do such a dangerous thing?"

It was a question that no one could answer, but I had a rather insidious thought. Before I could put it into words, Quin spoke.

"The spirits would have been called through the portal to this realm, either accidentally or on purpose. Both are possible, depending on the manner in which the portal was opened. As to why..." He shrugged and looked to me. "Cara, you have something to say?"

"I have a dreadful feeling about this." I swallowed.

"As do I," Jack ground out. Hannah rested her hand on his arm.

Quin arched a brow at me. "The book has gone missing," I told him.

"Missing!" He said something in French. My knowledge of that language was quite good, but I didn't understand it. Going by the vehement way he spat it out and Jack's blush, I guessed it to be something that shouldn't be repeated in front of ladies.

A soft knock on the door announced the entrance of the footmen, come to remove our dishes and supply us with the main course. They rolled in a trolley laden with platters of roasted meats and vegetables that they proceeded to serve. Quin looked as if he would combust if they didn't leave soon.

Once they wheeled the trolley out again, he ignored his food and turned to me. "We discovered it missing only a few days ago," I told him. "We think Myer hypnotized Samuel's lawyer to steal it."

"Then we'll find Myer and threaten him until he returns it."

Jack cleared his throat. "By threaten, you mean harm?" Quin leveled his gaze on Jack. "Thought so. I have no objections."

"It might not be Myer," Hannah reminded her husband. "Faraday is the one who's missing. His disappearance at the same time as the book is too much of a coincidence for me."

Quin's jaw hardened at the mention of Nathaniel. "I agree with Mrs. Langley."

"Please, call me Hannah."

"Hannah, I think you're right. It's likely Faraday took the book, came here and opened the portal."

"Why would he do that?" I asked. "He has no reason."

"That you know of."

I shook my head. "I still think Myer is responsible. The fact that Samuel's lawyer was hypnotized is a dead giveaway."

"Really, Cara." Sylvia clicked her tongue. "Do we have to use the word dead at the dinner table?"

I rolled my eyes at Hannah and she smirked back. "My apologies, Sylvia. I'll keep such gruesome words for the drawing room instead."

Sylvia narrowed her eyes, unsure whether I was teasing or not.

"There is something else Cara hasn't mentioned," Langley said to Quin. "Lord Alwyn had to be hypnotized to stop him from causing problems for her family."

"What kind of problems?" Quin asked me tightly.

"He decided the book must be valuable, since so many people were after it," I said. "He wanted it back. When I refused, he said he would hurt one of my loved ones. I didn't give it to him, and as it turned out, I couldn't anyway."

"He killed her father before Samuel could find him and hypnotize him into forgetting the whole thing." Sylvia was too intent on dissecting her beef to notice the effect her words had on Quin.

His bright eyes searched my face, his brow plunged in concern. He rested his hand over mine, and it wasn't until that moment that I realized I was trembling. My tears hovered close. I hadn't cried since hearing of François's death. I had not loved him, hardly known him, and tears felt like a waste. But now, under Quin's scrutiny, I wanted to cry for the man who'd fathered me.

He lifted my hand to his lips and kissed the knuckles. His fingers skimmed lightly down my bare arm, leaving a trail of goosebumps in their wake. The gesture was far too intimate for the dinner table, but I didn't care.

Quin really was here with me again, and I would make the most of his presence.

Mr. Langley cleared his throat and Quin let go. He concentrated on his food, but neither he nor I contributed to the rest of the conversation as the others tossed around their thoughts as to who had the book and why they'd used it to open the portal.

I was restless for the remainder of the evening and was glad when everyone dispersed to their respective bedrooms for the night. My restlessness only increased, however. How could I sleep when he was just down the hall?

I gave up trying when the distant chimes of the grandfather clock all the way downstairs announced midnight. I slipped out of bed and threw a wrap around my shoulders. I was beyond caring about propriety. Coy games would only waste the precious time we had together.

The carpet along the hall deadened my footsteps. Even so,

he wasn't surprised to see me when he opened the door upon my soft knock. Neither of us carried candles or lanterns, but I was close enough that I could make out the spark of interest in his eyes as his gaze swept over me.

"You shouldn't be here." His low voice rumbled in his chest, but there was no anger in it.

"I can't sleep. Nor can you, I see. May I come in?"

He hesitated then opened the door wider and stepped aside. The guest bedroom was similar to my own, with a canopied four poster bed taking up most of the space, a deep armchair positioned in the corner, a dressing table, and another small table and chair by the window. He closed the door, shutting out what little light had filtered through the window at the end of the hall.

His silhouette moved to the mantel where he lit candles. They provided enough light for me to see him, and admire. He wore only his leather pants—no shirt—and his hair was a little messier than usual. The muscles in his shoulders bunched then relaxed before he turned to face me, hiding the scars on his back from view.

I swallowed. It was easy to come to his room unannounced. Far harder to work up the courage to speak. All the questions I had for him simply vanished from my head and I was left with emotions rioting inside me.

"Sit," he said, indicating the armchair.

I did and he sat on the other chair. "At least you can sleep in a proper bed this time and not on a rollaway truckle."

He looked to the bed. "I feel like I'm sinking when I lie on it."

"They didn't have mattresses in your lifetime?"

"Not on campaign. Most of my adult life has been spent fighting in one battle or another, far from home and a soft bed. It will take some getting used to."

Here was another small piece of the Quin puzzle, albeit a

tiny one. If he'd been away so much, who cared for his estate? How often had he seen his wife?

I didn't want to throw those questions at him. It used to be easy to ask him things, only to have him bat them away without answering, but this time I couldn't. It felt too awkward between us.

I searched for something else to talk about instead. "Thank you for your help at the ruins today. I'm sorry I wasn't very understanding about removing Malborough's soul. You're right in that he would have been difficult to pin down if he'd moved. You had to act immediately."

"Destroying ghosts is harder for me than destroying demons. Demons are stronger, but at least I can see them."

"I'll try to be more help next time and direct you."

He nodded. "Tomorrow we'll travel to the other house and send the rest of the spirits back."

Would it really end so quickly? Tomorrow seemed much too soon. I found myself hoping the spirits had dispersed further afield.

"I'm sorry to hear of your father's death," he went on.

"Thank you, but we weren't very close. I've seen very little of him in recent years." I bit my lip. He probably knew all of that. He'd once told me that he'd asked the administrators all about me and been given some details of my life.

He tapped his thumb on his thigh and didn't meet my gaze. It would seem I wasn't the only one feeling awkward about this meeting. "I'm sorry Faraday has gone missing," he eventually said.

"I do hope he's all right. Perhaps he simply decided to leave London. It isn't as if he needed to inform any of us of his plans."

"That's not what I meant."

I cocked an eyebrow. "Then what do you mean?" I didn't know why I asked—I knew exactly what he was implying.

"He wished to court you. I thought perhaps you wished it too."

"Don't be ridiculous," I blurted out. All my awkwardness suddenly vanished. I couldn't have him thinking that Nathaniel and I were lovers. "I don't want to be wooed by the likes of him, and I'm surprised that you think I do. Besides, I kissed you mere weeks ago, Quin. I am hardly the sort of girl that kisses other men so soon after such a profound experience."

His eyes had grown wider and wider as I spoke, but now he leaned his elbows on his knees and lowered his head between his shoulders. Hair fell across his face, obscuring his eyes. He blew out a measured breath, then two more, before finally straightening. "Cara, I didn't expect to return here to you, and certainly not so quickly."

I waited for him to go on, but it was some time before he continued.

"I want to apologize for my lack of chivalry. I should not have taken advantage of your tender feelings."

"*My* tender feelings? I seem to recall you having feelings for me too. At least, your kisses would imply as much."

"My feelings are unimportant."

"Why?"

"Because dead men have no future in this realm, and dead men confined to Purgatory aren't allowed the freedom to feel. It's a luxury for others."

"That may be the case, but you *do* feel, Quin. You feel and you want."

"But I cannot have." His gaze arrowed into me, pinning me.

My fingers curled around the armrests, digging into the thick brocade. I stared at him until he looked away and leaned forward on his elbows again. My heart kicked, restarting. I hadn't been aware that it had stopped.

"You should go," he said heavily. "Meeting like this is not helpful for either of us."

I licked dry lips and willed him to look at me again, but he did not. "I...I came to ask you about those scars and how you got them. Will you tell me?"

He shook his head. "There's nothing to say. I deserved them. You know why."

My fingers clawed at the fabric as I pictured the scene. I shuddered and shut my eyes against the crack of the whip. The only way to banish it from my thoughts entirely was to talk about something else.

"You're married." Perhaps it wasn't the wisest thing to bring up at that moment, but I could truly think of nothing else. The knowledge of him having a wife had been infused in my brain ever since learning about it. It would have come out eventually.

At least it got him looking at me again. "How do you know?"

"I read about you in one of Mr. Langley's history books on the crusades."

He straightened, the movement slow, as if he were delaying his answer. "I was married, true. In another life."

"Your only life."

He conceded the point with a nod.

"Her name was Maria," I said. "You wed when you were very young. Or young by our standards."

"What else did your book tell you about her?" It was a simple enough question, but the steely edge to it was unmistakable.

"Nothing. What was she like?" *Did you love her?*

"I don't want to discuss her."

I looked down at my hands. "I was only trying to understand you a little better. I'm sorry."

"You won't understand me by asking questions about her any more than I will know you by asking about Faraday."

"Oh. Right. I see." I think. Was he implying that he *didn't* love her? Or was I reading something into his words that wasn't there?

I must have looked a little dumbfounded, because he chuckled. "What else did you learn about me from this book?"

"That you were born in 1164 and died in Jaffa, during the third crusade. One of your brothers fought alongside you and also died in the Holy Land."

I paused at Quin's flinch. His entire body seemed to tighten and twitch before relaxing again.

"I'm sorry," I whispered. "That was callous of me. I shouldn't be speaking about your loved ones as if you'd simply left them behind in another country. They're—"

"Dead. Aye, they are, and a long time ago. I don't wish to discuss them either. So what else did your book tell you?"

I tried to think, but it wasn't easy. I was still reeling from the brisk dismissal of his family. "King Richard bestowed a knighthood on you and considered you a confidant."

"We were friends."

"You make it sound like an everyday thing to be friends with a king."

He laughed. "Perhaps not quite friends, but we fought alongside one another and got drunk afterward. Many times."

"Got drunk? And here I thought you slew dragons and rescued damsels in distress on your white stallion."

He pulled a face. "Your book contains some errors if it stated that."

I laughed until I had to wipe tears from my eyes. "I'm sorry. It's just a modern day fantasy. Reality must have been too gruesome for the storytellers. You'll find that medieval knights have been romanticized over the years. Quite a few ladies would swoon if they found out what you were."

"Is swooning a good thing?"

"Only if you're there to catch them, otherwise it's a wasted effort."

He smiled. "Do you swoon?"

"Never."

"So now you know about my life. What else did the book say?"

"That's all. I do plan on reading it further, just to learn about the crusades themselves. My history of the era is sketchy."

"Perhaps I should read it too. I might learn something."

I grinned. "Thank you, Quin, for not getting mad at me."

"I admit it feels strange that you know these facts about me, but it's only fair since I know so much about you."

"That's what I told myself when I tried to justify it. And I didn't learn much anyway. I still have so many questions."

"Save them for another time. You should go back to bed. We'll both need our wits about us tomorrow." He stood, dismissing me.

I stood too. On impulse, I kissed my fingertips then touched them to his cheek. "Good night, Quin."

"Good night, Cara."

* * *

"YOU'RE NOT COMING." It was the third time Jack had said it to Hannah since we'd arrived in the dining room for breakfast.

She regarded her husband over the rim of her teacup. "Why not? Give me a good reason." At least it was a different response to "Yes, I am" which she'd given twice already.

"It's too dangerous."

"I'll remain in the coach."

Jack slathered butter on his toast then lifted it to his mouth. "Still too dangerous." He took a large bite, his gaze on his wife the entire time.

"I might be of some assistance."

He swallowed. "From the coach?"

She set her teacup down with a loud *clank* in the saucer. I concentrated on cracking the top of my boiled egg and pretended I couldn't hear them squabbling. It made me uncomfortable. Jack and Hannah were like Emily and Jacob, one of those rare couples with the perfect synchronicity of a Swiss clock. I hoped Jack knew that he shouldn't stifle such a vibrant spirit as Hannah. Although I did agree with him that she should stay out of danger, I suspected she was only insisting as a kind of test, to see where his boundaries lay.

"Would you prefer that I sit here and sew all day?"

"What's wrong with sewing?" Sylvia asked. She'd been silently tucking in to her bacon and eggs, and I'd thought she hadn't been listening. Her gaze had been on Tommy the entire time as he rearranged the way the sideboard was set up with our food. Although the footmen had brought the dishes in then left, Tommy had remained. He'd taken one look at the sideboard, shaken his head, and had been moving things ever since.

"Nothing is wrong with sewing," Hannah said. "It's just that I can't do it all day or I'll go mad."

"There's always painting," Sylvia suggested. "Or sketching."

Hannah stared hard at Jack over her cup. He blinked back at her like a trapped animal. "St. Clair, help me out here."

Quin stood by the sideboard, piling his third helping of bacon onto his plate. He paused, bacon dangling from the tongs over his plate, and regarded Tommy, of all people. Everyone except Tommy noticed. "I think you will be needed here more, Hannah, as lady of the house. You too, Sylvia," he added with another pointed look at Tommy.

Sylvia took a moment longer than the rest of us to gather his meaning, but once she did, she said, "We'll discuss what is to be done after breakfast, shall we?"

Hannah nodded. Jack smiled at her and she scowled back. "Just so you know, I am aware that I've been manipulated," she told her husband. "But I do agree with Quin."

"As do I," Jack said quickly. "But let me assure you, my darling wife, that I don't think boredom is a good enough reason to put your life in danger. I love you too much to watch you walk into a nest of ghosts who are intent on harming the living."

Her face softened and she smiled in return. It would seem the argument had ended, for now.

"Well done," I muttered to Quin as he sat down with his full plate. "You successfully solved a marital debate and have almost solved the problem of Tommy."

"The latter is still to be determined," he whispered back. The others were chatting freely once more, and did not seem to be listening to us. "As long as Sylvia and Hannah treat him as a man ought to be treated, it will be resolved."

"How should a man be treated?"

"Like he still has something to offer, even if he only has one good arm."

"Do you think that's why he keeps interfering in the servants' work? Yesterday I overheard the new butler complaining to Hannah that Tommy constantly finds fault."

"I believe so. I've seen it happen in my lifetime. A man loses his hand and he can't plow the field or hold a sword. Something inside him dies."

"His self-confidence. The worth he places on himself," I clarified when he gave me a blank look at the modern term.

"Aye, perhaps that's what it is. When others see that he has something else to offer that doesn't require two hands, then he feels he still has worth. Dawson needs to feel the same way. At the moment he doesn't know what else he can offer the household, but when he does, he'll be himself again. The ladies will find something of value for him to do, I'm certain of it."

"Quin, you are quite the modern thinker, for all your medieval attitudes."

"If my friends had known my opinions would one day be valued, perhaps I wouldn't have been so derided in my lifetime."

"That's rather unfair of them. In what way were you derided?"

"For treating servants as friends, and women as having value outside the kitchen and bedchamber. I could never understand why a woman who was as clever as a man couldn't own the gown she wore or speak her mind. I was fortunate, and sometimes unfortunate, to have known women with minds sharper than many men's. My own mother built up my father's estate to become one of the most successful in the county. He was too busy fighting."

"And your wife?"

"She was clever too," he said shortly, piercing his bacon with his knife. "Considerably more than me."

He didn't seem interested in expanding on that point, so I let the conversation drop. I watched him out of the corner of my eye as he finished his food then picked up his teacup in both hands. He'd not yet mastered an elegant way to handle the delicate china with his large fingers, and he looked as if he were drinking from a bowl.

"Do you have a plan of attack?" Jack asked him during a lull in the conversation. "If Emily were here we could have been assigned a medium each and attacked both the front and back of the house at the same time, but we can't do that with only one."

Quin shook his head. "You're not coming either."

"I bloody well am."

Quin set down his cup. "As you note, there is only one medium. There is also only one sword."

"And my demon-forged blade."

"Will you be able to get close enough to a spirit to cut open its chest?"

"If I have another weapon in my other hand, yes." Jack snapped his fingers and fire danced on the tips. I rarely saw him display his gift for fire so openly, but I suspected he considered himself to be among friends and safe. I also suspected he did it to impress Quin.

Quin seemed intrigued at first, but then merely shrugged. "A few flames won't worry a ghost."

"I don't want to worry it. All I need to do is distract it." He shook his fingers, extinguishing the fire. "Occupy it with one weapon, cut it open with the other."

Sylvia tutted. "Honestly, Jack. Can't you leave this discussion for later?"

The angles of Quin's face shifted into hard, unforgiving planes. "You are not coming, Langley. The only reason I'm allowing Cara to go with me is so she can direct me. You aren't necessary."

"Oh dear," Hannah muttered. "This isn't going to end well."

It was a little like watching two gladiators clash—neither was willing to give in, each as capable as the other.

"If it will just be the two of you, who will drive the coach?" Jack asked.

"I will," Quin said.

"So if you get into difficulty and must flee the scene, you expect to be able to outrun ghosts who can simply reappear wherever they want, gather up the reins, ensure Cara is on board too, and drive off again?"

I refrained from telling him that I was capable of ensuring I was on board all by myself. My interruption probably wouldn't be welcomed by either man.

"If you come, it's another person I must protect. I cannot be everywhere."

"Precisely. For one thing, I can take care of myself, and for another, who will remain near Cara and protect *her* if a spirit gets past you?"

Quin's lips pinched into a bloodless line. His nostrils flared. After a moment he released a sigh and gave a single nod.

Jack smiled. "I'm glad we see eye to eye."

I thought appealing to Quin's protective instincts was a low blow. It was, perhaps, his only weakness.

"You will not get in my way."

Jack held up his hands and nodded. He was still smiling.

"And you will not get yourself injured or killed."

"It's not on my agenda for the day."

Their boundary-setting was interrupted by Tommy storming out of the dining room. I hadn't been watching him as the two men argued, but I did catch the strained look on his face as he left. I suspected he was upset that he couldn't help too. For someone who'd been involved in protecting Frakingham and its occupants through many battles, it must be frustrating for him to not be able to do so this time.

Sylvia got up and followed him. Nobody asked her to wait.

After breakfast, we dispersed briefly to freshen up before leaving for the Tudor house. It had begun to rain and I thought a sturdy umbrella might be of use, not only to keep dry but to use as a weapon against the spirits if they got too close. Tommy would know where to find one so I went in search of him in the service area. I also wanted to see if he was all right.

It took some time to locate him, and Sylvia also seemed to have disappeared. The housekeeper suggested I look in the cellar, since Tommy had mentioned fetching some wine for dinner, much to the new butler's annoyance. I did find him down there, but he wasn't alone. Sylvia was with him, and they were kissing.

CHAPTER 6

My gasp caused them to spring apart. Its echo bounced off the low ceiling of the cellar and lingered a moment before finally fading away. I stared at them. Tommy avoided my gaze and shuffled his feet, but Sylvia approached me. Her face was ablaze, her lips swollen from Tommy's kisses. She touched trembling fingers to them.

"I was...we were just..." Her hand fluttered down to the choker at her throat. Her gaze slipped away. "Uh..."

"Looking for some wine?" I suggested. I was still in a bit of shock, but not quite as much as Sylvia appeared to be.

"Yes," she said weakly. "Wine." She cast a glance at the rows of bottles in the rack near Tommy.

Tommy withdrew one without glancing at the label. He didn't look quite so keen to pretend, but he went along with it, perhaps for her sake.

Sylvia touched her hair self-consciously. "Thank you, Dawson. I'll see you in the drawing room at ten." To me, she said, "Hannah and I have some thoughts on Tommy's future here at Frakingham that we'd like to discuss with him."

It was more information than I, as a guest, needed to know. I suspected she felt compelled to prove how normal everything was, how she was still a lady and Tommy the footman. Except it could no longer be that way. Their kiss changed everything. I could see it in her eyes as well as his. There was uncertainty in them, but mostly I saw something that I'd seen in Emily and Jacob's eyes many years ago. A sense that they'd found the thing they'd not known they'd been searching for. It was impossible to return to the life they'd led before the kiss, no matter how much Sylvia pretended otherwise.

I only hoped she didn't hurt Tommy before she came to that conclusion.

She marched up the stairs without looking back. Tommy wasn't quite so eager to leave. He approached me. The scars on his face weren't so noticeable in the dim light of the single lantern, but they were still a bald reminder of how close he'd come to losing his life to save the people and home he loved. "If Langley finds out about this," he said quietly, "Sylvia will be in trouble."

"I won't say a word. But as her friend, I must caution you."

He bristled and I worried that I was about to overstep the mark. But I had to say what was on my mind. She *was* my friend, and a somewhat naive one.

"Please give serious thought to the consequences before you engage in amorous endeavors again. You must consider whether this is a boulder you wish to push down the hill or not. Because if you do, you won't be able to stop it."

"Wise words," he said through a tight jaw. "Perhaps you ought to take your own advice." He walked off up the stairs too, his pace a little slower than Sylvia's.

"My situation is nothing like hers," I said to his retreating back. "You and she at least have a chance."

He didn't say anything, just kept climbing the stairs. I

grabbed the lantern they'd left behind and followed, wondering how he'd known I had feelings for Quin.

* * *

I NEVER DID FETCH AN UMBRELLA, but the rain eased before we reached the lane that led to the Tudor house. It had stopped entirely by the time we pulled up to the gate. I peered through the coach window, but there was no one in the front garden, living or dead.

Quin jumped down from the driver's seat and opened the door. He lowered the step and assisted me out. "We decided that you will sit beside Jack and direct me from there. That way he can drive off quickly if necessary and you are out of harm's way."

I glanced at Jack. He had the decency to look sheepish. "Do I not get a voice?"

"No," they both said.

I sighed. "And here I'd called your thinking enlightened this morning, Quin."

The corner of his mouth twitched, but the smile was so fleeting that I wondered if I'd imagined it. "It's for the best."

"For me, yes, but how will I be able to direct you from up there? I won't be able to see the ghosts at all."

"I'll lure the spirits out of the house."

I wasn't so sure that it was a foolproof plan, but I doubted I'd sway him into allowing me to go with him. He took my hand and assisted me up to the driver's seat beside Jack. As he turned to go, I grasped his shoulder. "Please be careful. If it gets too dangerous, you must leave."

He nodded and walked off through the front gate. I was about to tell him that he'd gone far enough, when he shouted, "Come out, Redbeard! I have a proposition for you."

"Redbeard is the leader?" Jack asked me.

I nodded, not taking my eyes off the house.

"Come out, coward!" Quin called again.

Still nothing. He looked back at me. I shrugged and shook my head.

"I need to investigate." I was about to climb down when a spirit suddenly appeared. "Quin! Straight ahead, at the bottom of the steps!"

He drew his sword, but remained where he was. The steps were too close to the front door, and too far from me, for my liking.

"You there!" I called to the spirit. "Come closer. We need to speak."

"You're that medium," he called back. He was a tall, solidly built fellow with midnight-black hair that fell past his shoulders in limp, oily streaks. He wore a jerkin of indeterminate color beneath all the blood, and matching wide pants that ended at the knee. Half a ruff formed a semi-circle around his neck, the other half probably having been blown off along with that side of his face.

"And you shouldn't be here," I countered. "You've already crossed over."

His lips peeled back from his teeth in a sneer, or what was left of lips and teeth. "And how do ye' know that, Ghost Girl?"

"I spoke to a gentleman haunting Frakingham Abbey. He told me that he'd crossed to a dark place then been called back to this realm. I know you were with him, but he chose not to join you here."

"He was a coward. A weakling. He ran home with his tail between his legs." He spat on the ground. "Tell him that from us when you see him again."

"We won't be seeing him again. Nobody will, in this realm or any other."

The ghost's jaw slackened and he blinked at me.

Quin carved a semi-circle out of the air with his sword,

catching the spirit's attention. His fists curled at his sides and he whistled.

"Three more have appeared," I told Quin. "Directly behind the first."

Jack swore softly and gripped the knife resting on his knee tighter.

"Where's your leader?" I asked. "The fellow with the red beard. Is he here?"

"He ain't our leader," snarled a spirit with a hole in his stomach. I could see clear through him to the other side. "We got no leader."

"Oh? It's just that he seemed like your spokesperson when we arrived yesterday."

"He's busy elsewhere." Half Face's hollow chuckle implied he was busy *causing problems* elsewhere.

"So it's just the four of you?" I asked.

I received no answer. Did that imply that they were alone, or that others were inside the house, staying out of sight until needed?

Quin beckoned the ghosts with his free hand. "Come closer."

"That sword a special one?" asked a fat ghost with the purplish coloring of a man who'd choked to death.

I didn't answer him. I could also play the not-talking game.

"You think he can fight four of us when he can't see us?" Half Face snorted. "Not likely."

So there were only four. I still didn't want Quin to get closer to the house, but if the spirits didn't move down the steps, he would have to. I gripped onto the small iron rail at the side of the driver's seat and told him to advance.

He did and the four spirits finally stepped down onto the overgrown path. Three of them advanced slowly, but the fourth, a pimply youth with prominent, equine features, ran at Quin.

"Prepare!" I called out. Quin settled into a balanced fighting stance, his focus dead ahead. "Strike...*now!*"

Quin sliced his blade right to left, but the youth jumped clear at the last moment. He whooped and danced, turning circles on the spot. The back of his head had been caved in. His brown hair was matted in the blood.

"Two feet to your right," I said, lowering my voice to a level that I hoped would still carry.

The instruction was hardly out of my mouth when Quin cut through the ghost's chest. The youth gasped and looked down at himself. There was no blood, but the blade had made a clean line from one side to the other.

"Cara?" Quin asked as he reached out.

"A little to the left. There!"

The youth's dead eyes opened wide as Quin plunged his hand in and pulled out the ghost's soul. He crushed it to dust and the youth's body followed.

"Bloody hell." Jack's soft exclamation was echoed by the remaining ghosts, only much louder.

They all stared, mouths agape, at the pile of gray dust scattered in the grass and leaves. One even crossed himself.

"Fool," muttered Half Face with a shake of his head. "Come!" he said to his companions. "Let's end this."

The other two spirits disappeared then reappeared almost immediately, with swords in hand, close to Quin. They slashed at him, but he parried both blows easily and danced away. The presence of the swords meant he could now locate the ghosts without needing me to direct him. The battle came down to speed. How quickly could he deflect their blows then cut them open and pull out their souls?

"Both are right-handed," I told him. Knowing that would not only help him with the angles and directions of his opponents' slices, but also tell him the approximate location of their chests.

He parried another two blows, one after the other, then had to leap out of the way of a fast descending blade. At the edges of my vision, I saw Half Face take a step back, but he remained on the front porch, also watching the fight. It was difficult to read his expression due to his wounds, but his gaze followed Quin's moves intently.

The two other spirits seemed to have realized they needed to use their ghostliness to win. They had two advantages over him that I could see. One was their endurance. Ghosts couldn't tire, and Quin eventually would. The other was that they could disappear and reappear wherever they wanted.

The fat one did just that, suddenly turning up behind Quin.

"Behind you!" both Jack and I shouted.

Quin swiveled, slashing in an arc. Sword, arm and body were one graceful yet violent motion. But his effort missed its target. Fat Ghost blinked out just in time and turned up beside Stomach Hole. He laughed as both plunged their blades at Quin at the same time.

Quin leapt backward, out of the way. We didn't need to give him directions for him to realize one of the ghosts was once more behind him. He swung around and slashed, catching Stomach Hole's arm.

Stomach Hole gasped and stumbled back. He inspected his arm and swore loudly. An ordinary blade would have no effect, but it seemed an otherworldly one could hurt. The blow wasn't enough to stop him, however. He rejoined Fat Ghost and both lunged in synchrony, once more.

Quin dodged both blades easily enough, but did not immediately attack.

"The fellow on your right is injured, upper right arm," I

called out. He didn't acknowledge me and I didn't want him to. He had to maintain focus.

"I don't know if I'm making a difference at all," I told Jack. I felt useless. The fight could drag on for hours, until Quin either tired or got injured...or worse.

"You're not the only one feeling that way," Jack muttered. "Take this." He rested his hand over my fist, bunched on my knee. The metal of his small knife was cold through the leather of my glove. "Use it if necessary."

"But you'll need it if you wade in. Which, by the way, I think is a bad idea."

He reached under the seat and pulled out a long, curved sword. It looked like one of the ones that hung on the billiard room wall of Frakingham. "It's not going to harm either of them, but it will keep one of them occupied while St. Clair destroys the other."

"Have you ever used a sword before?"

"I've fenced a few times."

"A few times!"

He shrugged. "How difficult can it be?"

I spluttered a protest, but he simply stepped past me, handing me the reins as he did so.

"Keep them steady," he said. "If the horses get spooked, just hold on."

"I know how to drive."

He dropped lightly to the ground and joined Quin, immediately striking at Stomach Hole. What he lacked in finesse, he made up for in sheer strength and speed. Stomach Hole was forced into a rose bush. Then he disappeared.

"Jack, behind you!" I shouted as Stomach Hole reappeared.

I directed the fight from the coach as best as I could, but I was no conductor and this was no orchestra. As soon as Quin or Jack got the upper hand, the ghosts would suddenly disappear and reappear elsewhere, often behind their opponents, sometimes to the side. It could not go on in such a manner if the ghosts were to be defeated. Quin and Jack would tire eventually.

They knew it too. That must have been why they reorganized themselves to stand back to back. They spoke in low tones that didn't reach me. In that formation, there was nowhere they couldn't see, no way the ghosts' sudden reappearances could surprise them.

They engaged a spirit each, keeping their backs together, fighting as one unit. I hazarded a glance past them to Half Face and was surprised to see that he hadn't moved from the porch. Why didn't he help his friends? What was he waiting for? Perhaps there were no other swords in the house. A shorter weapon, like a knife, would put him at a disadvantage and expose him to Quin's soul-destroying blade, but a broom handle or other long wooden weapon would be easily broken.

Then he vanished. I scanned the garden, but he didn't reappear. I stood up and looked behind the coach and all around. Still no sign of him. I tightened my grip on the knife and sat again. A sense of foreboding settled in my chest.

"Half Face has disappeared," I called to Quin and Jack. "I think we need to end this very soon."

Fat Ghost laughed. "Got you worried, eh?"

"You should be," his companion added as he dodged Jack's blade.

Quin said something to Jack that I couldn't hear. Jack's lips moved, forming a curse word that I'd never heard him use. He shook his head, not in refusal but dismay. Then he turned, tossing his sword to Quin as he did so. He was unarmed.

I gasped, wanting to cover my eyes, but wanting to see how it played out at the same time.

I watched as Stomach Hole's blade slashed at Jack. Jack dodged, then created a fireball in his hands. Stomach Hole paused, clearly confused and somewhat mesmerized by the flaming ball.

Quin parried Fat Ghost's stabbing thrust with Jack's sword and lunged at chest height with his own. Fat Ghost squealed and dropped his sword. Quin kicked it away and tossed Jack's sword back to him so he could once again engage Stomach Hole.

Quin wasted no time in smashing his fist into his opponent's chest, pulling out the dark mass and crushing it. Fat Ghost's scream of anger and frustration lingered longer than his ghostly body and sent a chill racing up my spine.

Quin then turned on Stomach Hole. The ghost glanced around, clearly looking for help from Half Face. But he was alone. He couldn't beat both men and he knew it. Panic made his swings wild and his eyes wide, but he continued to fight. Jack and Quin separated, and Stomach Hole chose to fight the more dangerous opponent, Quin. Jack slashed at the ghost's body, hitting resistance each time. If he'd been alive, the blade would have cut him open. But since he was dead, it merely glanced off him without drawing blood. It did, however, hinder him. Jack quickly realized he needed to attack Stomach Hole's sword arm, forcing his thrusts off course.

Quin timed his sword's slice to coincide with one particularly strong blow of Jack's. Stomach Hole gasped and let go of the sword. He ran off toward the house. Quin and Jack couldn't see him, only his sword lying lifeless in the grass. I opened my mouth to give them directions, but a strip of cloth clamped over it, smothering my shout.

Above me, the mangled flesh and greasy hair of Half Face appeared. His mouth twisted into a sneer. "Quiet, wench," he snarled.

I let go of the reins and tried to pull off the hand holding the cloth, but I went right through him. I grappled with the cloth and tightened my grip around Jack's knife.

Just then, Redbeard appeared under the apple tree. He laughed at me then turned his attention to Jack and Quin who'd lowered their swords. Both had their attention on the house, not me. They had no clue there was any danger.

I struggled against the cloth, shouting through the gag and stamping my feet on the kick board.

Quin spun round. "Cara!" He set off at a run, Jack at his heels.

"Now!" Redbeard shouted.

A dozen ghosts appeared, including Stomach Hole, knives and rocks in hand. They didn't chase after Jack and Quin, but instead, threw their weapons.

CHAPTER 7

A rock pelted Quin on the shoulder and a knife glanced off his arm. Jack half-turned and deflected a blade, but another bit into the back of his thigh. He grunted but kept going, limping toward the coach. The ghosts ran to their fallen weapons.

Quin's face drained of color. "Cara! He has a knife!"

So did I. The sharp end of the spirit's blade pierced a hole in my jacket and dress, but met more resistance from the whale-boned cage of my corset. He grunted in frustration. I took the opportunity to punch Jack's knife at Half Face's chest, as hard as I could.

He let me go with a gasp of pain and horror. He glanced down at the gaping hole I'd gouged out of his chest and tried to cover it with his hands. But I simply reached right through into the cavity as Quin had done. My fingers touched something solid. It felt like a smooth, cold rock. There was little resistance as I pulled it free and squeezed.

I gathered the reins as Quin leapt up beside me. He took in the dust at my feet then glanced over his shoulder. "Duck!" he shouted at Jack.

Jack did so as a knife sailed over him and hit the ground just short of the coach. Several rocks slammed into his back and he stumbled forward, but kept running. Quin jumped down and deflected another knife with his sword, allowing Jack to pass. A ghost appeared in front of Quin, dagger in hand. He sliced in its direction, ripping through the body, and reached into the wound. He pulled out the spirit's soul and squeezed, deflecting yet another knife as it sailed toward him.

He ran backward, watching for more flying weapons as I kept all the ghosts in sight, including Redbeard. The big brute was no longer laughing. Jack climbed up beside me, and Quin stepped onto the ladder. I urged the jittery horses forward and we raced away from the house and spirits. The horses followed the road without me needing to direct them, so I was able to keep watch on our surroundings.

No ghosts appeared. Quin, who'd been hanging off the side of the coach, now joined us on the driver's seat.

"I should thump you," he growled at Jack.

I looked past Jack and frowned at him. "He helped you."

"He left you unguarded."

"He gave me his knife and I was quite capable of using it, thank you." I didn't tell him my corset saved my life. I didn't think he'd be inclined to forgive Jack sooner if he learned a few pieces of whale bone stopped Half Face's knife from cutting me.

"Mind if I say something?" Jack asked.

"No," Quin snapped.

"Go ahead," I said.

"There were many more ghosts at the end."

"Too many to count," I told him.

"And they seemed to have worked out how to defeat the two of us."

I nodded. "They kept their distance so that you couldn't

engage them in close combat then used whatever weapons were at their disposal."

"Where did they all come from?"

"Half Face fetched Redbeard, and I suspect they were with him. They clearly had formed a plan before making an appearance. I think he's their leader, despite what they said."

"Leader in deeds, if not quite in name," Jack agreed. "Do you think they would be useless without him?"

"Perhaps. Quin, what do you think?"

"I think Langley should have remained with you."

I sighed and chose to ignore him while he brooded. "How's your leg?" I asked Jack.

The wound at the back of his thigh was difficult to see, but his hand came away bloody when he wiped it.

"We'll take you directly to Dr. Gowan," I said. "I'm not delivering you to Hannah like that. Do you have any more injuries?"

"A few minor cuts and bruises." He rolled his shoulder, testing it. "Nothing of concern."

"Quin?"

"No."

He remained silent, simmering with barely controlled anger all the way to the village. While Dr. Gowan attended to Jack, Quin and I drove to the police station and spoke to Detective Inspector Weeks.

"You must keep everyone away from the Tudor house," I told him. "Perhaps spread the word among the village that it's too dangerous at the moment."

"Miss Moreau," he said with a slippery smile. "It's a pleasure to see you again. I'm sure Miss Langley and Mrs. Langley are happy to have your esteemed company at Freak — Frakingham House."

I resisted the urge to roll my eyes. "Thank you, Inspector. But, er, did you understand what I said? It has come to our attention that the Tudor house on the edge of the village is somewhat dangerous right now."

He arched his severe brows at me then turned to Quin. He seemed rather fascinated by Quin, and I could see he wanted to ask him where'd he come from and why he had a sword strapped to his hip. Quin had refused to leave it behind in the coach tied up outside.

"And why is that?" Weeks asked. "Sir?"

"This is Mr. St. Clair," I said, mustering my patience. "He's a guest of Jack Langley's. Mr. Langley was injured at the Tudor house," I went on, interrupting their handshake.

"Injured?" Finally Weeks was taking me seriously. "In what manner?"

"In the manner of…claw marks."

His ratty nose twitched. "Is it the same wild dogs that plagued Frakingham?"

"It could be." I didn't like to lie unless absolutely necessary. Hopefully my answer was suitably vague to worry him enough to do something about it.

"Curious." He frowned. "Perhaps that's what's been making noises at night here in the village, and breaking things."

Quin's hand passed over his sword hilt as if he were preparing to draw. "Breaking things?"

Weeks nodded. "Our very own windows in fact, and the street lamp outside. Indeed, this building has been targeted more than any other in the village."

I'd noticed the boards across the window, but not the smashed lamp.

"It's as if someone has a grudge against the constabulary," he said.

My gaze locked with Quin's briefly before flitting away. The sorts of dark souls that were sent to Hell would certainly have a score or two to settle with the authorities. The police force was new to England, formed after the lifetimes of many of the spirits I'd seen today, but there had been a form of law and punishment even in ancient times.

"Has anyone in the village been injured?" I asked.

"A few ladies have complained of intruders in the night, but we've not found any evidence of breaking and entering."

"It may only be a matter of time before someone gets hurt," Quin said.

"I agree with you, sir. Although I'm not sure wild dogs did the damage we're seeing here in the village." He nodded at the window. "I thought it was gypsies. Last time this sort of thing happened, they were camped outside the village."

"I don't think it's gypsies this time," I mumbled. It didn't seem fair to lay the blame on the doorstep of real people. Wild dogs near Harborough, however, were nonexistent.

"Whoever or whatever it is, we'll stop them before they do any more damage." Weeks seemed pleased with himself, even winking at me. "Isn't that right, Constable Jeffries?"

The baby faced constable looked up from his desk behind the front counter. "Pardon, sir? I wasn't listening."

Weeks sighed.

"Just keep everyone away from that house," Quin said. "We'll take care of the problem."

"Now, sir, I don't think it's wise to take the law into your own hands. I know it can be frustrating to let others take care of matters, but—"

"I said, we'll do it." Quin's voice was low, guttural, an unspoken threat threaded through them.

Weeks swallowed and backed up against the counter. "I can't condone the involvement of civilians in maintaining law and order."

"I'm not asking you to condone it. Just ignore it."

"We've dealt with them before," I assured Weeks quickly. "We know what we're doing."

Weeks gave an unconvincing nod. "With respect, miss, sir, if it is gypsies, you'd better get them to move on real soon. Any more of this and a mob will form and storm the Tudor house."

"Please, don't allow that to happen," I begged. "It's far too dangerous for ordinary folk."

"If you think I can control a mob then you're sadly misguided, Miss Moreau."

I sighed. "Just do your best, Inspector. For the sakes of the villagers."

Quin and I left. I climbed up onto the driver's seat as he untied the reins from the post. "This is quickly turning into a disaster," I muttered as he joined me.

"At least the ghosts haven't ventured too far afield."

"That we know of."

* * *

THE ENTIRE HOUSEHOLD must have been awaiting our return. Hannah, Sylvia and Tommy met the coach before it had come to a complete stop, while Bollard pushed Langley in his wheelchair onto the porch. They were all clearly relieved to see us again.

The three of us sat on the driver's seat, Quin holding the reins. Both men had refused to sit in the cabin while the other drove, and I didn't want to be alone. The journey had at least given us some time to discuss what to do next.

"We saw you coming from the tower window," Sylvia said. "What took so long?"

Jack climbed down, jumping the final foot or so and landing deftly on his feet. It was all an act for his wife's bene-fit. He'd limped out of the doctor's surgery.

"Jack!" Hannah cried. It would seem his ruse hadn't worked. "Jack Langley, you're injured! Let me look."

"It's nothing," he told her. "Just a scratch."

"A scratch that required Dr. Gowan to sew him up again," I told her.

Hannah gasped then scowled at Jack. Jack scowled at me.

I shrugged. "She ought to know."

Fray led the horses and coach around to the stables while we entered the house amidst a barrage of questions that came from all quarters, except Hannah. She was still too busy alternately scowling at her husband and embracing him.

"Before I begin, I need tea," I said as I headed to the drawing room. "Very strong tea."

"Tea isn't strong enough," Jack added. "Is it too early for brandy?"

"Yes!" Sylvia clicked her tongue. "You can drink tea like the rest of us, for now."

"After he has changed and I've inspected his wounds," Hannah said. Jack didn't object. Indeed, he looked rather pleased at the prospect of his wife fussing over him. He certainly needed to change to make himself presentable. Not only were his trousers ruined, but his waistcoat bore the marks of several dirty rocks that had hit him, and his shirt had come untucked. Neither he nor Quin had worn jackets, preferring the freedom of movement without them.

"If you'll excuse me too," Quin said. "I must change as well."

"Do you require assistance?" Tommy asked.

"Thank you, but I can manage."

"I'll fetch the tea then."

"You'll stay right here," Sylvia said, snippy. "You're no longer the footman, valet or butler. You're one of us."

Langley cleared his throat, which caused Bollard's usually blank gaze to switch to his master. The small lines around his eyes deepened.

I arched my eyebrows at Sylvia. "It appears you've made some changes while we were out."

Jack gave a firm, decisive nod. "Good. I'm glad. Save that discussion for my return."

He and Hannah departed, Quin having already gone ahead of them up the stairs. I watched his retreating back, wondering how severe his own injuries were. There was no blood on his clothing that I could see, and he seemed to be moving easily enough.

Sylvia looped her arm through mine and led me into the drawing room. "It's up to you to tell us what happened, Cara. And then we shall tell you all about our morning, won't we, Tommy?"

He nodded and tossed out a smile that lit up his face. It was good to see them both happy.

I told them about our morning fighting spirits, pausing only when the maid brought in tea and sandwiches. We'd missed luncheon and I was grateful for the food. Quin joined us, looking fresh in a clean shirt, though he wore no waistcoat, tie or jacket. His damp hair had begun to dry and curl at the edges, softening the severe lines of his face. He still moved easily enough, so I was quite sure he was uninjured, although there was a small scratch on the back of his hand and a faint bruise on his left cheekbone.

He tucked into the food, eating most of it before Jack and Hannah arrived so that Sylvia had to request more. I finished my recount by telling them that we'd warned Inspector Weeks to keep the villagers away from the Tudor house.

"That will only suffice for as long as the ghosts remain there," Langley said. He'd sat quietly in his wheelchair by the door as I spoke, not interrupting. It was difficult to tell if he'd been listening the entire time, or his mind had drifted off. Bollard stood beside the chair, his focus on the floor at his feet.

"True," I said. "We must hope that they see the Tudor house as some sort of base and remain there. It appears that they've wandered off now and again to haunt other avenues, but most have returned."

"And how many have left the group entirely to haunt elsewhere for good?" Jack asked. "Like Malborough."

It was a question none of us could answer. I didn't want to think about the possibility of countless evil-minded ghosts escaping into our realm. It was going to be difficult enough returning the dozens we knew about.

"We'll patrol the village," Quin announced.

We all looked at him. "How?" Sylvia asked. "You cannot be everywhere all the time. You both need to sleep."

"We should send for Emily," Hannah said. "That way you can share the burden."

I shook my head. "Not yet. Not until the situation worsens. She wants to spend time with her family over the summer. They're not far away. If we send a telegram she can get here in a day."

"The ghosts have not harmed any living soul," Quin added.

"Except for us." Jack tapped his finger against the side of his teacup. "But that doesn't mean they won't."

"The question remains," Langley said. "Why would they harm anyone? What do they have to gain?"

"That depends on what they want."

"To make mischief," I said. "To enjoy the time they have here. I think they understand they're back in this realm by accident and their time may be limited. For the majority of them, the people they knew have passed on and there is no one to seek revenge upon except the authority figures of our time, Weeks and his ilk. I believe they're here to have fun, or their version of it. We can only hope that killing and harming the living continues not to appeal to them."

"We'll rest this afternoon," Quin said to me. "At dusk we'll travel to the village."

"But you'll miss dinner!" Sylvia cried.

"We'll dine at the inn."

"If you must." She screwed up her nose. "But not The Red Lion."

"I don't like the idea of you wandering about in the dark, Cara," Langley said. "It'll be even more dangerous than the Tudor house."

"Thank you for your concern, but I have to do this. The situation is not ideal, but Quin will be there."

"And me," Jack said.

"No," came the almost unanimous response. Only Tommy and Bollard remained silent, and the latter because he couldn't speak.

"You're too badly injured," Hannah told her husband.

"I agree," I chimed in before he could protest.

Quin picked up another sandwich. "You'll be more a hindrance than a help."

Jack bristled. Hannah rested her hand over his. "I know it irks you, but you need time to heal. Quin and Cara will do a fine job alone. Not as fine as if you were with them, but they will come to no harm, I'm sure of it."

He narrowed his eyes at her. "It seems I have no choice."

"At least the weather is warmer," I said cheerfully. "Perfect for a little nighttime investigation."

My smile withered beneath Jack's cool glare.

Thankfully Hannah distracted him with an announcement. "Now, onto our news. Tommy has agreed to become Jack's assistant."

I clapped lightly. "Wonderful! I'm sure he'll do a marvelous job."

"The work was beginning to become too much for me anyway," Jack said. "I've needed an assistant for some time."

The pointed glance he shot at his uncle wasn't lost on anyone, least of all Langley himself.

He gave a curt nod. It would seem the matter had been discussed, and dismissed, before. "I'll leave the details up to you, Jack. Since you cannot assist Cara and St. Clair, you can spend time with Dawson."

"You should call him Tommy now," Sylvia said.

"He will always be Dawson to me." Langley signaled to Bollard to push him out. "I'll bid you all good afternoon. We have work to do. St. Clair, I'm relying on you to take care of my niece's friend. Beaufort will have both our heads if anything happens to her."

It was a rather empty threat since Quin was already dead, but everybody was too polite to point it out.

Jack and Tommy dispersed to discuss estate business, leaving Quin with us three ladies. Sylvia took up her sewing and moved closer to me, which took her further away from the window and the light. I waited for her to say something, but she did not.

Quin strode around the room, picking up journals, reading a paragraph then returning them to the table.

"Why don't you retire for the afternoon?" I suggested.

"What about you?"

"I will, soon."

"Then I'll retire when you do."

Beside me, Sylvia shifted and crossed her ankles. She didn't look up from her stitching. Hannah glanced up from the book she'd started reading, her gaze shifting between us on the sofa and Quin now standing by the window.

"Why not read about your exploits in the library," I told him with a wink and nod at Sylvia.

His gaze slid from me to her then back again. He nodded. "I've always wanted to know how history judged the crusaders." With a shallow bow, he exited the drawing room.

Sylvia blew out a breath and lowered her sewing. "Finally. Now, Cara." She turned to me. "It's been troubling me ever since our encounter this morning, but I do need to tell you that whatever you saw, or think you saw, didn't happen."

"Sylvia, that doesn't quite make sense. Did I see you and Tommy…er…?" I glanced at Hannah.

She smiled. "Kissing is the word I believe you're looking for."

"How do you know?" Sylvia cried.

"I guessed. You two have been cheerful all morning. Considering the dangers afoot, I thought it odd. I suspected something had progressed in your relationship, and that was the natural conclusion. Thank you for confirming it."

"That is unfair. You tricked me."

Hannah merely grinned. I bit my lip to stop myself smiling too.

"First of all," Sylvia began, "there is no relationship. Secondly, that is what I'm trying to tell you—there was no kiss."

A laugh spluttered out, despite me trying to hold it back. "It looked like a kiss from where I was standing."

"The light was poor," she said hotly. "I was merely comforting Tommy after he left breakfast in an unhappy mood. Nothing untoward happened, and I hope you won't spread rumors to the contrary."

"Of course not," I said, more serious. "You must tell your uncle when you're both ready."

She picked up her sewing again and I exchanged glances with Hannah. She frowned and gave a brief shake of her head. I suspected she thought as I did—that Sylvia might never be ready to tell Langley. Hopefully Tommy would urge her to broach the subject, and soon. It was only a matter of time before he realized that his niece and his former footman were kissing in the basement.

"Isn't it marvelous that he's Jack's assistant now?" I said. "I'm glad Mr. Langley saw fit to change his role."

Sylvia smiled. "Tommy was very pleased. We all are."

"It's a shame it took his injury to make August agree to the promotion," Hannah said with a sigh. "It was long overdue. Jack has been suggesting it for years, apparently."

"I believe Uncle August is beginning to soften and modernize. First the extra servants, then the ball, and now this. They're all good signs for a bright future here at Frakingham."

It was indeed, and boded well for when she did finally tell him about her relationship with Tommy. I hoped.

* * *

"Where do you think evil spirits spend their evenings?" I asked Quin.

"The police station," he said.

We'd just come from there. All had been quiet as Inspector Weeks locked the front door and left for home. "Where else?"

"The alehouse." Quin leaned against the lamppost and watched the front entrance of The Red Lion across the road. The pub's crimson door didn't look so bright in dusk's sepia wash, or the dozens of windows so bright. It resembled a sleeping giant, until the door opened and music and laughter momentarily escaped before being muffled again.

"This is the main pub in the village and all seems as it should be," I said. "So where else would they go?"

"To the bedrooms of beautiful women."

"Quin!"

He shrugged without taking his eyes off the inn, but I saw the curve of his lips as he smiled. "They cannot touch, Cara, only look."

"I know, but we shouldn't speak of such things. We shouldn't talk about them either."

His smile turned to a chuckle. "Modern ladies are excessively modest. I hadn't expected that."

"We are not all modest."

"Sylvia breaks out in a sweat when her ankles are accidentally uncovered."

"That's Sylvia. We are not all as prudish as her."

"Prudish." He repeated the word, sounding it out slowly as if testing its fit. "Show me your ankles then."

I lifted my skirts to the top edge of my boots. "There. Satisfied?"

His eyelids drooped heavily. He crossed his arms and stared down at my boots. "No."

I lifted my skirt and petticoat higher, almost to my knees. It was rather more leg than I was used to revealing, and I prayed no one was watching. Despite my reservations, I never backed down from a challenge. "What about now?"

He looked away with a sigh. "You made your point."

It wasn't an answer, but I let my skirts drop and they swished against the pavement. Clearly he was more interested in teasing me than admiring my legs. They were rather scrawny, I supposed, and I'd never liked my knees.

"Do you think we ought to find the most beautiful women in the village and keep watch?" I asked. "That could pose a problem since I don't know too many residents. The Butterworth girls are pretty enough, but Hannah and Sylvia would be considered prettier by everyone except Mrs. Butterworth."

"Hannah and Sylvia will be safe with Jack and Tommy. And you are here with me."

Heat swamped my face and my throat dried. "Oh. I…er… thank you. That's quite a compliment to include me with them."

"It's not a compliment, it's a truth." He pushed off from

the lamp without looking at me and seeing the effect his words had. "Let's check inside."

He was half way across the road before I gathered my wits enough to follow him. He opened the door to The Red Lion and I entered ahead of him. It was at that point I realized our evening might not go according to plan. We had wanted to patrol the streets and buildings anonymously, but it rapidly became clear that we were too conspicuous. My skin color, gender and clothing set me apart from the men drinking after a long day at work, and Quin's magnificent size and powerful presence meant he was equally difficult to ignore. Conversations dried up and heads swiveled toward us. One in particular caught my attention.

The nebulous figure dressed in prison-gray grinned.

CHAPTER 8

"We'll leave," Quin whispered in my ear. "I don't like the way they're looking at you."

The conversations resumed around us in a low hum and the ghost turned away. "We can't go. I've spotted a spirit near that table of dice players."

Quin rested a hand to my back and steered me toward the long polished counter. "Did he recognize us?"

"I don't think so. I didn't acknowledge him so perhaps he doesn't know I'm a medium."

"We'll soon find out." He ordered a glass of wine for me and a beer for himself from the landlord who'd helped us locate Malborough and the book of spells on Quin's last visit. He gave us a nod of greeting as he slid the drinks along the bar.

"Has there been any trouble here of late?" Quin asked him.

The landlord wiped his hands on the cloth slung over his shoulder. "Why do you ask?"

"Weeks mentioned some smashing of lamps and windows in the village."

"And what has that got to do with you?"

Quin's jaw tensed. His fingers tightened around the glass. "Just answer the question. I'm trying to help you."

The landlord considered this then leaned forward over the counter. "Some glassware was broken last night during a fight."

"A fight?" I whispered. "Is that a common occurrence?"

He looked offended. "No, miss, it ain't."

"Why did the fight start?" Quin asked.

He nodded at the dicing table. I followed his gaze and saw that the ghost was still there, his attention on the fellow rolling the dice. When the dice settled, he moved one with his finger. The man who'd rolled it accused his companion of bumping the table. Offended, the second man called the roller all manner of names in a loud voice, gaining the attention of most of the other patrons. The roller got to his feet, his thick black brows crashing into a frown. The name-caller slid his chair back and would have risen to his feet too except that a third man intervened and calmed them down by suggesting the dice be rolled again.

The spirit threw his head back and laughed.

"Some of my regulars are complaining of being unlucky here the last two nights. They're threatening to go elsewhere." He straightened and used the cloth to wipe the surface of the bar where he'd been leaning. "There's not much you can do about this place being unlucky, sir."

Quin gave him a tight-lipped smile. He picked up his beer and sipped. The landlord went off to serve another customer while Quin and I sat on stools near the door. I watched the spirit as he continued to affect the fall of the dice, always to the disadvantage of one particular player. That fellow grew angrier and angrier with each roll, and it was only a matter of time before he lashed out.

I didn't need to keep Quin informed. He could hear the

shouted accusations and responses of the rest of the patrons. I sipped my wine and Quin drank his beer. Neither of us spoke. I flicked my gaze around the room, being sure never to let it settle on the spirit. He was too intent on his own mischief to notice me anyway.

It wasn't a punch that started the fight. It was more of a lunge. After the man he accused of cheating spat in his face, the dice roller leapt at him, sending them both crashing through the ghost and onto the table behind. Wood splintered, glasses shattered and people scattered, only to regroup around the two men wrestling among the debris and spilled beer.

"Stand by the door," Quin said, rising. Jack's blade wasn't visible, but I knew it was still tucked up his sleeve, where it had been ever since we'd hidden the sword in the bushes by the stream upon our arrival in Harborough. "Where is he?"

"Behind the man with the long gray beard," I said as several more patrons joined in the fight. "No, wait. He's moved to the window where he can see better." I grabbed Quin's arm before he could walk off. "He moved again. You have to let me do it."

"No."

"Quin, you must. You can't see him. He's not holding anything to guide you. Either I come over there with you and whisper his location in your ear, which will look suspicious, or you give me the knife."

"Cara…" He sucked air between his teeth and let it out slowly, lifting his gaze to the ceiling. Then he slipped the knife from his cuff and tucked it under mine. The cool, hard steel was a comfort against my arm. "I will be right behind you."

He wasn't joking. He rested one hand on my hip and walked as close to me as my bustle allowed. We skirted the fight as best we could, although as more patrons joined in, the harder that became. The harried landlord tried to calm everyone down, but his voice was lost in the shouts and chaos. The fight spread from the corner of the dicing table and into the rest of the taproom. Already the room was a mess of tangled bodies and broken furniture. There was nothing we could do to stop it.

We approached the spirit without him even noticing, too intent was he on the original two opponents, still wrestling one another at his feet and sometimes through them. He whooped at a particularly vicious punch.

I removed Jack's knife from my sleeve, but didn't plunge it into his chest. "You there," I said.

Nobody took any notice of me, including the ghost. Quin's hand tightened on my hip. "Cara," he warned. "You cannot save them all."

"I can see you," I said a little louder.

A few men glanced at me and looked away when they saw I wasn't addressing them. The spirit stepped back, startled.

"You...you're *her*!" he said, staring at me. "They told me about you." He glanced past me to Quin and touched his throat at his grimy gray collar. "They said to beware of the medium and her lackey."

"You have to go back," I told him, keeping my voice low now that I had his attention. "Back to Hell or wherever it is you're from."

"I ain't going back there. It's a cruel place." He rubbed his throat again, pulling down the collar. A raw, red line had been burned into his skin. A rope would do that. He'd been hung.

"You have to," I said, steeling myself. "If you don't, my friend here will rip out your soul. Do you know what that means?"

"It means I won't exist. Not even in that dark place."

"That's right. So you have a choice. Return or have your existence ended."

He backed away and I was afraid he would disappear altogether. I shuffled the blade down so that the tip was now in line with my middle finger, hidden from view, but easily accessible.

"Stay back while I talk to this gentleman," I said to Quin over my shoulder.

His fingers flexed before letting me go. He even turned around and pushed one of the fighters back into the fray when he got too close.

I walked up to the spirit and whispered so that he had to lean in to hear me. "I can see that he makes you anxious, so let's leave him out of this, shall we?" He nodded eagerly. "You and the others won't win. Quin is an otherworldly warrior, and we possess several blades made in the demon realm. They're specifically designed to remove souls from ghosts." Not quite lies, more like an embellishment of the truth.

"But I don't want to go back," he whined.

"You either go back or have your soul crushed."

He glanced over my head at Quin and sighed. "If you'd seen that place, you wouldn't be giving me this choice." He nodded at the fight, still in full swing around us. "This…this is what I want—"

I stuck the knife into his chest. He screamed so loud that I felt sure everyone must have heard it. He gurgled something, his lips moving furiously, but no words came out. I withdrew the knife and pushed my hand through the hole. I pulled out the soul and crushed it. The dust turned into a gluey mass in the spilled ale near my feet.

I tucked the knife back up my sleeve and caught Quin's hand. I dragged him after me and out through the door. Dusk had surrendered to the night and I headed to the darkest spot on the street, away from the lamps. I still held

Quin's hand as I slumped against the brick wall of Miss Marble's Coffee House.

"I had to do it," I said, breathing hard.

He clasped my shoulders and rubbed his thumbs in soothing circles. "I know."

"But I'm not sure he deserved to have his soul turned to dust." My lower lip wobbled so I bit it. I did not want to cry in front of him. Not over this.

Quin cupped my face in both his hands. "Cara," he murmured. His honey-thick voice slid over me, caressing me as gently as his thumbs along my cheekbones. The tenderness brought my tears even closer. "You gave him a choice. I heard you. It's more than we gave Malborough or the ghosts at the house."

"I know. I think that's what bothers me. I gave him a choice and he still chose nothingness over Hell."

He kissed my forehead, his lips lingering for several aching thumps of my heart. "You did the right thing. Don't be sad. Not for these souls. They're bleak and cruel and deserved their fate."

I sighed and rested my head against his chest. He hesitated, then closed his arms around me. I felt rather than heard him sigh too, as his body relaxed against mine. A single, thunderous thump of his heart sounded against my ear. It never ceased to amaze me that he could be dead and yet have a functioning body.

"Are you sure you're not alive?" I murmured.

"I'm sure." He sounded like he was smiling. "I exist here temporarily, and I can cease to exist on this realm if my body dies. My soul will immediately return to Purgatory if I do, just as it will when this task is over."

I tilted my head and frowned up at him. "But...surely if you can die here, you can also live."

"The administrators of Purgatory have granted it so that I can complete their tasks when needed. But that's all."

I placed my hand over his chest. His heartbeat was so strong, his skin warm. It seemed impossible that he could truly be dead. Although my head knew it, my heart didn't want to believe.

"Cara." He brushed his knuckle down my cheek and gave me a sad smile. "You won't find the answer you seek. What you want…it's impossible." He dropped his hand, when I needed it to hold me, and turned away. His deep sigh lingered in the crisp air after he walked away.

I trotted to catch up and we walked side-by-side back to the stream. I didn't bring up his life, or death, again, even though I had questions and doubts. For one thing, if the administrators granted him the living body for temporary assignments, why couldn't they grant it to him forever?

By the time we reached the stream and collected the sword from its hiding spot beneath the bush, I'd calmed down somewhat. He was right about The Red Lion ghost. The man must have done despicable things in his lifetime to be sent to Hell in his afterlife, and I *had* given him a choice.

Quin removed his jacket, tie and waistcoat and spread them over the bush then strapped his sword to his hip. He looked every bit the avenging warrior, albeit a well-dressed one in trousers and shirt. He didn't ask for Jack's knife and I kept it tucked up my sleeve for safekeeping. I would probably need it again.

"Ready?" I asked.

He nodded and we headed back up the bank and across High Street to the shops. Nobody was about. Everyone was indoors, either at home or in one of the pubs. We could patrol the village without worrying about villagers seeing us.

"We'll head to the police station again," he suggested. "It seems to be a place they like to haunt."

I tried to think like a spirit who'd suddenly found himself out of Hell and back in the realm of the living. Where would I go? What would I do if all the people I knew were dead? I couldn't think of anywhere in particular to haunt. In fact, it struck me as a rather dull existence, but I suppose I wasn't maliciously inclined.

We rounded a corner and I paused, throwing my arm across Quin to stop him too. "There's two," I whispered with a nod at the police station on the opposite side of the road. "They're trying to pull off the boards protecting the broken window."

He squinted into the darkness. "I see the boards moving. Only two?"

"Yes. Come on."

He held me back as he scanned the area. "As long as those boards stay in place, they have no access to weapons."

"Then we'll be able to defeat them easily if I tell you where to strike."

"We risk them leaving as soon as they recognize us."

True. It was simply luck that the one in the pub didn't disappear. I looked up and down the street, and finally settled on a plan I suspected Quin wouldn't like. "You go back the way we came and skirt around to the rear of the police station," I said. "Hide in the shadows between that tree and the wall of the station. When you're in place, give me a signal and I'll pretend to be somebody out for an evening stroll. They won't recognize me in this light if I keep my face averted and I pretend not to see them."

"I take it I am to attack when they take an interest in you?"

"I'll draw them to your hiding place. Be sure to keep to the shadows until the last moment."

He hesitated. "There will be no chance to speak to them and give them a choice."

"I know," I said heavily. "But you're right. They're aware of us now and what we are here to do. If they're still on this realm then they've made their choice."

He withdrew his sword. "When you hear an owl's call, cross the road." And then he was gone, sprinting back down the road behind us and into a side street.

I kept to the shadows at the corner until I heard the owl a few minutes later. I couldn't see Quin at all, and I hoped it wasn't a real owl hooting.

I lowered my head and crossed the road. The blade's tip bit into the skin on my palm as I lowered it into position in my hand. My footsteps echoed in the darkness, catching the attention of the spirits. Out of the corner of my eye, I saw that they were two burly men with gunshot wounds in their chests.

"Here's somethin' tasty," one of them said, slapping the other in the arm. "Want to have some fun?"

"How?"

They considered what to do next as I drew closer. "We could lift her skirts."

The other one sniggered. I braced myself for their juvenile game. As my skirts lifted, I stopped, turned and glanced around, as any normal woman might do. The two ghosts laughed at their antics and went to do it again. I walked off quickly and they followed. The second time my skirts lifted, I was right near where Quin ought to be hiding.

I stopped again, scooped up some soil from beneath the tree and dropped it on the shoulders of the one who'd lifted my skirt. He frowned and went to brush it off just as Quin emerged from the shadows, grabbing the attention of both ghosts.

I plunged the knife into one as Quin cut through the chest of the soil-covered spirit. We both pulled out the dark masses of their souls and crushed them before either ghost seemed to realize what had happened. Their dust blended with the leaves and earth beneath the tree.

Quin sheathed his sword and dusted off his hands. "That was a clever idea."

"Thank you." I bent and scooped up some more dirt, filling my pockets. "For next time."

There was little need for talking as we patrolled the village. We came across another spirit at the railway station, placing stones on the tracks. The lure of a lone female again proved too much temptation, and he would have been easily led to Quin's hiding spot if I'd bothered to draw him in that direction. Since he was alone, I was able to remove his soul without Quin's help.

We picked off single spirits here and there as we encountered them. Some simply lounged about, staring up at the stars, looking bored, while others were in the process of emerging from windows after committing some sort of mischief.

"Those were numbers eight and nine tonight," I said as we dispensed with two spirits removing tools from the blacksmith's shop.

Quin tilted his head to the side, listening. I heard it too. A woman, screaming. The sound was faint, distant but unmistakable.

We walked quickly in the direction of the scream. By the time I reached the base of the hill leading up to the Butterworths' house, I was out of breath. I wished I'd left my corset on the bush along with Quin's clothes.

"I know these people," I said, grasping his arm to slow him down. "They'll think it odd for me to be walking around at night with a man."

"We'll keep out of sight."

The screaming had ceased, but we could still hear talking

and what sounded like someone crying. We deviated from the road and crept in the shadows of the trees instead.

"Someone was in there!" The frantic female voice hovered between shouting and crying. It came from the garden beyond the iron gates of the Butterworth house. "I swear on the Holy Bible, someone was in my room!"

A man's voice responded, too low and calm to be heard from where we crouched near the gatepost.

"I don't care if you've checked! Check again! I am not going into that house until the culprit is caught. Where are my girls?"

"Here, Mama," came another voice.

I peeked around the post and spotted the imposing figure of Mrs. Butterworth standing on the front porch, dressed in nothing but a nightgown with a shawl around her shoulders. Her husband held her by the elbows while her three daughters stood nearby. The two elder twins had their hair in curling rags and looked decidedly annoyed at having their sleep interrupted. Jane, the youngest, held a cricket bat as she peered out into the garden.

"I was not imagining things!" Mrs. Butterworth cried in response to something her husband said. "Am I in the habit of doing so? Am I?"

A footman dressed in a black jacket thrown over a night-shirt appeared in the doorway. He said something and Mr. Butterworth commanded him to look again.

"Someone was there," Mrs. Butterworth told her husband after the footman departed. "My bed linen was lifted right before my eyes, and then my nightdress too. I am not making it up or imagining things."

"Can you see a spirit?" Quin whispered.

"No. He may have gone." Just as I said it, a hazy figure appeared briefly at an upstairs window then disappeared. He reappeared on the ground near the family. "There's one now."

"What's he doing?"

"Watching the Butterworths. He's got his eye on the twins, I think."

Quin growled low in his throat. "Cur."

The spirit suddenly looked up at the window from which he'd jumped. "We had the wrong room!" he called. "The girls are down here now. We'll follow them when they go back inside."

My blood thudded in my veins, heating up with my rising anger. "There's another. They're after the girls," I whispered to Quin.

Two more ghosts suddenly appeared next to the first one. "Three now," I told Quin. I scrunched my fingers in the soil at my feet and shoved it into my pocket. "They plan on following the girls back inside."

"Damnation."

"How will we separate the ghosts from the family? We can't attack in their presence."

Quin didn't answer because I suspected he didn't know either.

The curtain fluttered at the upstairs window and another spirit faded in and out as he emerged onto the sill. "I'm goin' to enjoy playin' with those two lassies," he called down to his friends. He threw his head back and laughed. His red beard shimmered in the moonlight.

CHAPTER 9

"*R*edbeard's here too," I told Quin. "What shall we do?"

"We wait. When the family returns inside, we must find a way in and stop Redbeard and the others."

"But they'll lock up the house. We can't go around breaking windows and sneaking in. We'll be discovered."

He remained silent for a long time, perhaps contemplating his options. When the footman returned and spoke to Mr. Butterworth, Quin swore under his breath. "There is no alternative."

I watched the family closely. Mrs. Butterworth appeared to be the only one up in arms about an intruder. Her husband was trying to placate her by having the footman search the house, but I suspected he didn't believe her. Her elder daughters looked bored, and her youngest paid them no mind at all. She stood on the bottom step, facing the garden, her gaze scanning the fence line. She was the only one looking our way.

On impulse, I stepped in front of the gate as her gaze

swept past. Quin grabbed my hand and dragged me back into the shadows.

"What are you doing?" he hissed.

"Getting Jane's attention."

"Who's Jane?"

"The little girl. She knows me. She'll probably let us in."

"Why would she do that?"

"Her head is full of fanciful notions." Jane was ten years old with an adventurous spirit. Where the members of her family were rather silly and irritating, she was whip-smart and lively. She could also keep a secret. "She'll believe me when I tell her we're hunting evil ghosts. Look at her. She clearly thinks her mother isn't imagining things."

He followed my gaze to Jane who was now approaching the gate at the end of the drive. Her family took no notice of her. "I still think it's a terrible plan."

"At least it is a plan. Have you got a better one?"

He merely grunted.

"Miss Moreau?" whispered Jane. "Is that you?"

"Yes," I said, revealing myself to her before stepping back into the darkness again. "Jane, I have something very important to ask of you."

"Is it spies? Were they after my mother?"

"No, not spies."

"Not that Myer fellow?" She wrinkled her nose.

"No. It was ghosts."

"Ghosts!"

"Shhh."

But it was too late. Her father had heard her. "Jane? Come away from there."

"I'm just picking flowers," she called back. She plucked a rose from the bush. "We don't have long," she said to me, all seriousness. "Tell me about the ghosts."

"They're intent on doing harm. Quin and I must stop them."

She peered past me, scrunching up her eyes and nose at Quin's outline, just visible beside me. "He's a very large fellow."

"With special powers that send evil ghosts back to the afterlife."

"You can see them, can't you?"

I nodded. "Jane, I need you to unlatch this gate. Then you must leave a door or window open for us to get inside the house. We have to stop them before they do harm."

Her father called again. When she didn't answer, he stepped down from the porch.

"Quickly, Jane," I whispered. "You must decide now if you will help us. But please, even if you decide not to, you must not tell anyone that you saw Quin or I here. Do you understand?"

Mr. Butterworth strode up the drive. "Jane! Come here! Now. We're going inside."

"Jane?" It was difficult to convey urgency in a whisper, but I must have managed it, because Jane turned to her father.

"Coming," she called. "Just one more flower." She picked another rose, unlatching the gate as she lifted the flower to her nose. Then she trotted back up the drive and slipped her hand into her father's.

They returned to the porch then all five of them went inside. The footman closed the door. The click of the locks were loud in the silence.

The ghosts lounged on the porch, waiting. None had shown any interest in Jane's wanderings, and I was convinced that we hadn't been seen.

Quin stood close behind me, his heartbeat thumping out a steady rhythm against my back. It seemed to take forever for the ghosts to disappear. Once they did, I could picture them, wandering through the house, looking for the twins' bedroom. I grew restless, watching, waiting for Jane to open a door. It seemed to take forever.

It wasn't the door she opened, however, but a window. An upstairs one. I groaned.

"There's a pipe running alongside the ivy," Quin said. "I can climb it."

But could I?

We swung open the unlatched gate and crept into the garden. We avoided the gravel drive and the grass muffled our steps. With the ease of a monkey, Quin climbed the pipe, occasionally using the ivy to leverage himself up. I studied the pipe. Perhaps I could do it. I was contemplating where to place my foot when the window nearest me opened.

I jumped back into the shadows and flattened myself against the wall, but it was only Jane.

"Psst," she hissed. "Come in this way."

The ground floor window was more accessible, although I still managed to snag my skirt and land awkwardly in the room beyond. Jane helped me to my feet.

"This way," she whispered, grabbing my hand. "I saw my sisters' door open but no one was there."

We tiptoed up the stairs and I silently thanked Mrs. Butterworth for decorating them with a carpet runner. There wasn't enough light for me to see by, but Jane seemed to know her way in the dark. I allowed her to lead me and we met Quin in the upstairs hallway.

"Which is their bedroom?" I asked Jane.

I could just make out her silhouette pointing at a door. If the ghosts had opened it, then they'd closed it again after entering. They were inside, doing God knew what to the girls. It would only be a matter of time before one or both of the twins awoke and screamed. The entire household would once again be in uproar—and we would be the first to be blamed for violating the girls.

I let go of Jane's hand and headed toward the door, but Quin held me back. "Jane, light those candles."

She took the three-pronged candelabra and disappeared into another room.

"Cara, I'm going to open that door then move down the hall to where you'll be hidden from view."

"You're going to draw them out into the light?"

"I hope so."

Jane returned, the candle flames flickering with each step.

"Place them on that table," Quin whispered, nodding at the semi-circular table against the wall opposite the twins' door. She did. "Now return to your room and shut the door."

"But I want to help."

He leaned down to her level and met her gaze with his own steady one. "You've played your part perfectly. Now you must allow others to do theirs."

She nodded solemnly.

"Do you understand the need to keep this a secret?"

"Of course." She sounded offended. "I've been keeping secrets my whole life."

"Good. Now go."

She disappeared into her room and shut the door. I withdrew the knife from my sleeve and moved into the darkest part of the hall where my black skirts and hair would blend into the surroundings. Quin unsheathed his sword then turned the door handle. He quickly moved to join me as the door swung open.

"Someone's there," came a voice that must have belonged to one of the spirits.

"Who cares?" I recognized the Scottish accent of Redbeard.

"Nobody's there," said a third. "Go on, let me look at her again."

"If nobody's there, who opened the door?" asked the original voice.

"Ghosts?"

The men laughed.

"Look at all that skin," crooned one. "What I wouldn't give to be able to touch it."

I shuddered and shook my head at Quin. He frowned back at me. Then he knocked on the wall.

"Jesus Christ!" bellowed one of the spirits.

"Told you someone was there."

"Go and see," growled Redbeard. "I don't want my sport interrupted again."

A ghost suddenly appeared in the hallway outside the door. I nudged Quin in the shoulder but didn't dare speak. He knocked on the wall again, softer this time.

The ghost squinted into the darkness. "Who's playing tricks?" he asked. "That you, McIntosh, you old prick?" He walked toward us, still squinting. "I know there's someone there."

"In line with the bottom edge of the painting," I whispered. "Now."

The spirit heard me, but it didn't matter. Quin was too fast, his strike too accurate. He'd turned the ghost's soul to dust before he had a chance to open his mouth and scream.

We didn't celebrate. We crouched again and Quin once more knocked on the wall.

"Bloody hell, Dickson!" shouted Redbeard. "I thought ye were going to scare the kidneys out of 'em!" When he received no response, he said, "Dickson? Christ, go and see what games he's playing."

Another ghost emerged and we lured him with the same trick, sealing his fate in the same manner.

Quin resumed his knocking. Amid a flurry of cursing, Redbeard himself appeared. The fourth ghost emerged from the bedroom too. At least we'd drawn them away from the sleeping twins.

"Both near the door," I whispered to Quin.

Redbeard cocked his head to the side. "Somebody there? Dickson?" When there was no answer, he nudged his friend. "Go and see what they're doing. I'm bored with their pathetic games."

The other ghost mumbled something under his breath and came toward us. "Same height as the first one," I told Quin. "Now."

He slashed his blade through the air, slicing a gash across the ghost's chest. I didn't wait to see Quin crush the soul. I ran down the hallway at Redbeard.

"Cara!" Quin hissed.

I kept running. Redbeard's eyes flared wide, his jaw fell open. But he recovered from his surprise before I reached him. He grabbed the candelabra and threw it onto the floor. "Bitch!" he spat. He disappeared.

Damnation! Redbeard was gone and we'd been heard by the household. Footsteps pounded through the house. Mrs. Butterworth screamed and her husband shouted orders. Quin grabbed my hand and dragged me away from the scorched carpet.

But there was nowhere for us to go. Footsteps thumped on the stairs. We were trapped.

"In here," hissed Jane from her doorway.

Quin pushed me into her room then followed. She shut the door and leaned against it.

"Hide behind the curtain." She shoved Quin. "Quickly!"

The curtain was made of thick, heavy brocade that reached the floor, easy to hide behind. As long as nobody looked there.

But Quin had other ideas. The window was open. When I looked out, I realized it was the same one he'd climbed through. He took my face in his hands and forced me to look at him.

"Can you manage it?"

"Of course." I had to. The house was about to be searched from top to bottom. We needed to get out.

"I'll go first."

"To catch me if I fall?"

I could just make out his smirk in the moonlight. He climbed through as Jane's door crashed back on its hinges. I urged Quin to keep going, but he hesitated. I could see he was worried about me being left behind. But if one of us was to be discovered in Jane's bedroom, it was better that it be me and not him.

I flapped my hands, urging him to go. He began to descend.

"Jane!" snapped Mr. Butterworth. "Jane, are you all right?"

"Yes." She sounded sleepy. The bed creaked and the linen rustled. "Papa? What's wrong?"

"Your mother and I heard footsteps and a crash. There's a candelabra outside that's fallen onto the floor."

"Oh," she said. "I put that there."

"Why?"

"I was frightened after Mama thought she heard someone. I wanted some light in the hallway in case I needed to leave my room in a hurry."

Her father clicked his tongue and gently lectured his daughter on the dangers of leaving a naked flame unattended. I was fully out of the window, my feet secure on the pipe when he asked her if she'd heard any other noises.

"Only you and Mama shouting. You woke me up."

I didn't hear any more of the conversation. I concentrated

on finding footholds on the pipe, and when I couldn't, using the ivy.

Until the ivy came away.

Curses! My foot searched for a hold, but found nothing solid. The pipe was smooth in that section, and I no longer trusted the ivy. I looked down and saw Quin climbing back up to me. He raised his hand, palm up, offering me a platform. I tentatively placed my boot on it then more of my weight. He made no sound as I put my entire weight on him.

I continued to climb down, using Quin as a ledge twice more. With only a short jump to the ground remaining, he grabbed me around my waist and lifted me down. I grasped his shoulders as he lowered me gently, my body against his, our gazes locked. His bright eyes searched mine and my heart stopped. He was going to kiss me.

"You shouldn't sleep with it open," came Mr. Butterworth's voice above us.

We flattened ourselves against the wall beneath the window. There was nowhere else to go. I closed my eyes and prayed he didn't look straight down.

"I forgot it was open," came Jane's voice just before the sash was slammed shut.

Quin grabbed my hand and together we raced away from the house and out the gate. We paused in the shadows near the gatepost. I sucked air into my lungs while Quin watched the house.

"It's safe," he said. "We weren't seen."

"Do you think Redbeard will be back?"

"I don't know. We'll wait and see."

He leaned his shoulder against the tall iron post and kept his gaze on the house. I kept mine on him. If he thought about kissing me again, he gave no indication. I might as well have not been there. He didn't speak to me, didn't look at me.

After a while I sat on the ground. My dress was already

dirty and torn anyway. I leaned my head back against a tree trunk and closed my eyes.

I drifted off. I don't know how much time passed, or if I fell asleep. A soft noise nearby had me suddenly reopening my eyes. Quin crouched in front of me, a startled look on his face. He recovered quickly and stood.

"We should go." He held his hand out to me.

I took it and together we walked down the hill toward the center of the village. "Were you watching me as I slept?"

"I was checking that you were still breathing."

I snorted a laugh. "I didn't over-exert myself *that* much."

"That contraption you wear under your gown resembles a torture device. It wouldn't surprise me if it cut off your airways."

"I should have left it at the house. It's supposed to make my waist slender. You don't like the effect?"

"Your waist is slender enough."

"Thank you, Quin. Now what do we do?"

"It's late. Or early. You need to rest."

"I'll be perfectly all right. We should patrol the village again, just in case Redbeard is taking his frustration at being interrupted out on someone else."

"Very well."

We reached the blacksmith's shop, but all seemed quiet. "Your plan worked marvelously," I told him as we continued on. "We managed to destroy three spirits at the Butterworths' house."

"But not Redbeard."

"We'll get him next time."

"We work well together."

"We do," he said. "But you should leave Redbeard to me."

"You were occupied with the other spirit. I had to act."

"He could have hit you with that candelabra."

"Or I could have dodged his swing and gone in low with the knife."

"Is that so?" He sounded like he was smiling, although his lips were perfectly straight. "That would have been quite a move."

"It's one I picked up off you. The only reason I didn't do it is because he didn't try to hit me. I think he wanted to burn the place down, only the carpet was woolen and the flames went out."

We walked together in silence for a while and I thought the conversation over until he said, "Leave Redbeard to me next time, Cara."

"I will. If I can."

He sighed but did not make me promise. I suspect he knew it would be an empty one anyway.

We wandered through the village for a few more hours until Quin declared it was time to rest.

"Not yet," I said. "They could be waiting for us to leave."

"Cara, you're tired. You need to sleep."

"I just need to sit down for a few minutes." My legs ached and my toes were swollen, even though my boots were the most comfortable I owned. "We could rest here on the banks of the stream near your clothes."

"Very well."

We sat together, our legs stretched out on the grass. After a moment Quin lay on his back and linked his hands over his stomach. He stared up at the stars. I lay down beside him and assumed the same position, albeit more awkwardly thanks to my bustle.

"They're the same as I remember them," he said quietly.

"The stars?"

"Aye."

"You studied them?"

"Only as much as anyone who traveled studied them.

They helped guide us when we sailed to distant lands. Witches used them to tell fortunes too."

"There are no such things as witches."

"Is that so? And who says this?"

I shrugged. "People."

"The same people that don't believe in ghosts, mediums and demons?"

"*Touché.*"

He was quiet a moment, then said, "The stars are the only constant. Everything else in this world is different from my lifetime. People, houses, the way you speak and behave. I didn't recognize London. Even the countryside has fewer trees and more villages."

"It must be unsettling."

"It is strange when I stop to think about it." He turned his head and smiled at me. "But I'm too busy to think beyond the task at hand when I'm here. Perhaps that's a good thing."

"There are a lot of spirits to remove before you can return to…that place. You could be here for some time."

He sighed. "I hope so."

I blinked at him, but he turned to gaze up at the stars again. "Is there no possible way you can remain here?"

"No, Cara," he said heavily. "There isn't." He closed his eyes and after a few minutes his breathing slowed.

I inched closer to him until our shoulders touched then closed mine too.

* * *

"Cara." Quin's murmured voice rumbled from his chest to mine.

I opened my eyes as my hair was lifted off my face and swept back. I was lying half on top of Quin, my head tucked beneath his chin, my hand over his heart as if I'd been feeling its rhythm in my sleep. Birds flicked leaves off the ground, hunting for worms, and weak sunlight filtered through the trees on the opposite bank of the stream. It was dawn.

Quin sat up, drawing me with him. I yawned and stretched to cover the fact that I missed touching him so intimately. He stood and helped me up.

My hair fell across my face again. I touched it and realized it was as messy as it always was when I awoke. Most of the pins had come loose and thick ropey curls hung to my shoulders. I tried to fix it, but without a mirror I suspected I did a poor job.

In fact, I knew I did a poor job from the amused look Quin gave me. "Here," he said, plucking a leaf from my hair. He removed leaves and pins, handing the latter to me. When he finished, he ran his fingers through the strands, teasing out the tangles. "I like it better this way."

I glanced at him over my shoulder and caught the tail end of his small smile as he concentrated on his task. He stopped as soon as he noticed me looking. I sighed at the loss of his touch.

He put on his waistcoat then plucked his jacket off the bush and offered it to me. "Are you cold?"

I accepted it gratefully. The air was a little chilly, although the day promised to warm up with the lack of breeze and clouds. I settled the jacket around my shoulders as he tucked his tie into the waistcoat pocket.

We headed back through the village. There was no one about, living or dead, and we decided to return to Freak House. We headed to the police station stables, where Weeks had allowed us to lodge our horses overnight. Quin pushed the stable doors open.

Inside, a ghost sat on a bale of hay at the rear of the building. He was dressed in a clean nightshirt, his face starkly pale and glossy. He had probably died from a fever.

"Good morning, Miss Moreau," he said in clipped, cultured tones. "I've been waiting for you."

"How do you know my name?"

Quin withdrew his sword. The ghost put up his hands in surrender. "Don't kill me." He chuckled at his pun.

"How many?" Quin asked.

"Just the one." I glanced around, searching for more spirits. If this was an ambush, we were easy targets.

"I'm alone," the spirit said.

He seemed to be telling the truth, although there could be others hiding in the stalls. There were six in all, but only four were occupied by horses. I pushed on the nearest door. It swung back, startling the gray. There were no ghosts inside.

"You could check each one," the spirit said. "It would bring you closer to me, which is what you want anyway."

I eyed him up and down. He'd been middle aged when he died, with an open countenance and soft, round face and paunch. But as we drew closer, his eyes became hard and his smile turned to a sneer.

"So, Miss Moreau, have you guessed who I am?"

I shook my head. "Just another ghost who should be in Hell." I felt for my knife, still tucked against my forearm.

"True. But I prefer to go by my real name. Percy Harrington." He bowed. "You may call me Master."

 stared at the ghost of Percy Harrington, the man who'd tormented Charity during his lifetime and after his death. He was linked to the Myers through Edith Myer, his heir. He'd also possessed the body of one of his business rivals, nearly destroying the poor fellow's business and reputation. He was not a nice man.

"What is the name of the medium who helped you possess?" I asked him.

Beside me, Quin, adjusted his grip on the sword, drawing Harrington's gaze.

"So impatient." Harrington clicked his tongue. "Youth these days. And anyway, that's not the question I want you to ask me."

I gritted my teeth. "What do you mean?"

"Keep trying. Go on. Ask me another." He gave me a slick smile and sat on the bale of hay again.

"Stop playing games, Harrington," I said for Quin's bene- fit. "What are you doing here?"

"Better," the spirit said. "But still not the right question." He leaned back against the brick wall and crossed his arms.

"You know, you *are* a pretty one. So different to my Charity, of course, but no less pretty for all that. Indeed, you rather complement one another. Light and dark, day and night. You would have made the perfect pair."

My stomach rolled. The man was sick. "Tell me what you want, and then get out of my sight."

"Or what? He'll remove my soul?" He nodded at Quin.

It was my turn to smile. I would not let this man think he had the upper hand, even if he had thrown me off-course. "He may not remove it here and now, but he will get to you at some point. You'll become nothing, Percy Harrington. You will cease to exist."

"Save the dramatics for the ignorant ones. I don't need your lecture. I know what will happen to my soul if he uses that weapon on me. I'm not a fool like them. I know that any existence is better than none."

I shook my head. "I don't understand. You came here to tell me you're returning to Hell? Why?"

"I thought you were clever, but that's still the wrong question." He sounded bored. "Keep asking. You'll get the right one eventually." He waited, a smug smile on his bloodless lips.

I resisted the urge to grab the broom and smash the smile off his face. Instead, I relayed the conversation to Quin. Doing so helped me form my thoughts.

"You want me to ask you *why* you're here," I said to the ghost. "Not just you, but all of you."

He clapped slowly. "Very good. Top of the class. No strap for you today."

Bile rose to my throat. I swallowed it down. "Well?"

"Well. Myself and the other spirits you've been seeing hereabouts were the lucky ones—or unlucky, depending on your view—who were wrenched from Hell one hot day."

"Wrenched?"

He shrugged. "I can think of no other word to describe it. It was like being sucked through a tunnel. One moment I was sweltering in Hell and the next I was here. At the Frakingham Abbey ruins, as a matter of fact. I recognized the place from the time I possessed that fool, Clement. My fellow black-hearted souls and I had been spat out of the eye of an intense local storm."

"The portal," I muttered.

"Was it? Well. I knew instantly that something wasn't right. Souls that have crossed over shouldn't come back. Anyway, as I gathered my scrambled wits, I noticed someone inspecting the storm. He couldn't see us. As I watched, he climbed into it. He, and the storm, disappeared."

"My God. Someone willingly entered the portal? Can you describe him?"

"I can do better than that. I recognized him. It was Everett Myer."

"Myer!"

"Cara?" Quin asked without taking his gaze off the bale of hay.

Harrington chuckled. "I'd wager he loathes not being able to see and hear me while you can. Men like that hate feeling inferior, particularly to women."

It was my turn to chuckle. "You're wrong, Harrington. Men like you are the ones who feel inferior. Isn't that why you spent a lifetime hurting them? To make yourself feel stronger, smarter?"

His nostrils flared and his razor-sharp gaze shredded me. There were more things I wanted to say to taunt him, but I refrained. Angering him further might make him change his mind and decide to stay and haunt us.

I quickly told Quin what Harrington had said.

"Why are you telling us about Myer?" Quin asked when I finished. "What do you gain from it?"

He shrugged. "I don't like him. I'm happy to cause him problems."

I relayed his answer to Quin, then said, "How do we know you're not making it up?"

"You have to trust me." He shot me a dazzling smile that turned him from cruel to handsome. It was easy to see how Charity had been duped in the beginning, if he used that smile on her.

"So you're leaving now?" I asked him. "You'll return to Hell?"

"I will. I won't risk having my chest ripped open and my soul crushed to dust. I rather like it, black thing that it is." His smile turned wolfish. "Goodbye, Miss Moreau. Be sure you don't grow too attached to your creature."

"Wait!" I stepped forward, but Quin grabbed my arm, holding me back. "How many of you are there?" I asked Harrington.

"Dozens," he said cheerfully. "Enough to keep you busy for some time. But I suspect if you destroy their strongest, the Scot with the red beard, they'll all return to Hell. He's keeping them roused and entertained. Remove him and they'll simply grow bored."

"Are they at the Tudor house now?"

"No. You frightened many of them this last night. They've dispersed."

"Damn."

He clicked his tongue. "If you were mine, I would put you over my knee and thrash you for your foul language."

"Go!" I growled. "Go back to where you belong."

He laughed. And then he was gone.

I scrubbed my hands over my face and blew out a long breath. "He left," I told Quin.

The hand he placed on my back was reassuring. "Did he say anything else?"

"Only that the ghosts have fled the Tudor house. He didn't say where they went."

"Do you believe him about Myer?"

"It seems plausible that he would have found the book, opened the portal and gone through. He's certainly curious enough."

"And foolhardy."

We prepared our horses in silence. I knew few details of Charity's life with the master, and now that I'd met him, I was relieved not to know more. She was the bravest person I knew to have walked away from his clutches and kept her sanity. If I hadn't thought it before I did now.

We rode out of the village, not toward Frakingham House but in the direction of the Tudor house. It was silent, inside and out. The only sounds came from the birds and our horses' hooves. Redbeard and his men had indeed gone.

* * *

I SLEPT all morning and awoke in the early afternoon when Inspector Weeks called at the house. He told us that the Butterworths had reported an intruder, but nobody had seen who it was and the family were unharmed.

"I'm sure it had nothing to do with the wild dogs at the Tudor house," he said with a twitch of his nose. "Do you agree, Mr. Langley?"

"I'm sure you're right," Jack said.

"Fortunately the police station incurred no further damage last night. It would seem your patrolling of the vicinity worked, Mr. St. Clair. I hope you didn't keep Miss Moreau out too late."

"It wasn't really patrolling," I told him. "More of a leisurely stroll on a pleasant evening."

Weeks's gaze slid from Quin to me then back again.

"Indeed. What modern sensibilities you young people have. Walking about in the dark alone would never have been allowed when I courted Mrs. Weeks. Of course, she wasn't Mrs. Weeks then."

Sylvia cleared her throat. "Would you like to stay for tea, Mr. Weeks?"

"I'm sure the inspector is a very busy man," Hannah said with a hard glare at her cousin-in-law.

Jack steered Weeks to the drawing room door with a hand at his back. "We wouldn't want to keep you, Inspector."

"Quite right," Weeks said as Bradford appeared to show him out. "I'd best get back. It was a pleasure to meet with you all. Mrs. Weeks will be thrilled when I describe the ladies' outfits to her and tell her I was invited to stay for tea."

"Another time," Sylvia said with a smile.

"Please let us know if you hear of any other strange goings on in the village," I said. "Anything at all."

Weeks nodded and made his exit. I sighed and slumped back against the sofa. Hannah smothered a laugh. "I see he hasn't changed."

"Still the sycophant," Jack agreed.

"I don't mind him," Sylvia said. "He's well mannered. Quin, you're very quiet."

"I'm thinking about Myer." He stood by the window, staring out at the front lawn and beyond, to the abbey ruins and lake. "And whether Harrington told the truth."

I'd been thinking about him too. We'd reported back to Jack as soon as we'd arrived at the house, and he must have informed the others while we slept.

"I think we need to go to London and speak to Mr. Myer," I announced.

"You can't," Jack said. "You're needed here to round up the ghosts. Quin too. I'll go. I need to make some business calls anyway."

"We will both go," Hannah corrected him.

It was settled that they would leave in three days, after Jack had introduced Tommy to the tenant farmers and shown him what to do. He already knew the gamekeeper and Frakingham farm staff.

Quin and I patrolled Harborough again that night, but there were no spirits in the village or at the Tudor house. The next day we asked Weeks to telegram the neighboring village constabularies and ask if more crimes than usual had been reported. By that evening, when we returned for our third nighttime patrol, he reported that there'd been none.

"I think Harrington was right when he claimed the ghosts have vacated the area," I said after we'd done an entire lap of the village and found nothing out of sorts.

"Aye, but where did they go?"

I yawned and pulled the collar of my coat up to protect my neck from the wind. It whipped up High Street, rattling the glass lamps and tugging at my skirt. The air smelled of pending rain.

"I'm taking you inside," Quin said. "You're going to fall ill if you spend the night out in this."

"And you won't?"

"I'm hardier, remember?" He took my elbow and steered me back the way we'd come. "We'll see if we can get rooms at The Red Lion."

* * *

THE FOLLOWING DAY, we checked in with Inspector Weeks. The village had slumbered peacefully during the night. We detoured via the Tudor house, but it too was empty. Nothing had been disturbed there in three days.

We were on our way back to Frakingham when Constable Jeffries met us on the road. "Miss Moreau!" he called as he reined his horse to a stop alongside ours. He handed me a folded piece of paper. "I was at the post office when a telegram arrived for you. I knew you'd just left so I offered to deliver it. I'm glad I caught up with you. Saves me some time."

"Thank you, Constable."

He touched the brim of his hat then rode off back the way he'd come.

I read the telegram. "It's from Samuel. He wants us to come to London if we can be spared here. 'I have news on Faraday' it says." I showed it to Quin. "I wonder if he's turned up."

"Faraday might be able to tell us what Myer was doing climbing into the portal." He pretended to read the telegram, but I knew he watched me from beneath lowered lashes. "I'm sure you're relieved."

"Of course I am. I thought something might have happened to him, or that he took the book." I plucked the telegram from his fingers and tucked it into my coat pocket. "That's as far as my interest stretches. Indeed, call it curiosity more than interest. He could answer some burning questions we have. That's all."

"You're rambling, Cara."

I made a miffed sound through my nose and urged my horse forward. I didn't know why he was teasing me about Nathaniel. I thought I'd made it clear I had no interest in him.

Quin caught up to me and we rode in silence for a while. "I do want to go to London, more than ever," I said. "But Jack doesn't think we should go."

"He'll change his mind when we tell him there are no spirits here."

"I wonder where they went."

"Mayhap Faraday can tell us that too."

* * *

WE GOT rooms at Claridge's Hotel on Brook Street, London, since I didn't want to stay in Emily and Jacob's house while they weren't there. It was closer to the Myers' house than Samuel's so Quin and I decided to walk to Berkeley Square after depositing our belongings at the hotel. Jack and Hannah had other matters to attend to.

"Mr. Myer is not at home," intoned the butler. "Would you like to leave a card?"

"Is Mrs. Myer here?" I asked on impulse.

"She's indisposed at the present time."

So she was in, but didn't want to receive visitors. "Please inform her that Miss Moreau and Mr. St. Clair have news about her husband. We'll wait here while you do so."

He hesitated, clearly unsure whether it was worth disturbing his cantankerous mistress or not. He was saved by the woman herself.

"It's all right, Adamson," she said from the top of the stairs. "I can spare a few minutes for Miss Moreau and Mr. St. Clair."

Adamson bowed and retreated from sight. Mrs. Myer descended the stairs, her brown skirts skimming the carpet. She did not offer to take us through to the drawing room. Indeed, she didn't even smile in greeting, but then again, she rarely did. The few smiles I'd seen her bestow always seemed somewhat sinister to me. She regarded first me then Quin with eyes that were deceptively lackluster, hiding the shrewdness I knew lurked there.

"You mentioned having news of my husband."

"We do," I said. "Of sorts. We had hoped it wasn't true and that we'd find him here."

"He's been gone for some time."

I exchanged a glance with Quin. "Have you searched for him?" he asked.

"Not as yet."

I frowned. That was an odd response. "Have you reported him missing?"

"Phhhttt. The police are useless. Besides, I'm sure Everett will turn up."

"He goes missing often?"

She glanced at the clock as it chimed four. "Would you mind getting to the point of your visit, Miss Moreau? I haven't got time for this."

Even when discussing such a worrying topic, she could still be as blunt as an axe. "We've been told that your husband was seen entering the portal at Frakingham Abbey."

Shock rippled across her face, draining it of color. Her tongue darted out, licking her bottom lip, and her hand fluttered at her throat. For someone who always seemed so bland, it was a lot of movement. "I told you to destroy that portal," she spat. "You should have listened to me." Her vehement response surprised me. Did she worry about her husband only because she knew, or suspected, he'd entered the portal?

"Why should we listen to you on the matter of the portal?"

Quin's question brought the color back to her cheeks. She swallowed. "Who saw him enter it? Perhaps there's been a mistake."

"We're not at liberty to say."

"Mr. St. Clair, I am simply trying to establish whether your source is a reliable one."

I tugged on my jacket hem, a nervous habit of mine. I hated that this woman made me anxious. There was really no reason for it. She'd never harmed me. "It was a spirit, as it happens. When Mr. Myer opened the portal, some ghosts were wrenched from…from the afterlife and brought here."

I thought she might mock me, or disparage me. She hadn't always been accepting of the supernatural and those who believed in it, particularly her husband. She'd made it quite clear that she thought his obsession with the paranormal a waste of time. But she accepted my answer with a cool nod.

"And this particular ghost described my husband to you?"

"He knew him. It was Percy Harrington."

She linked her hands in front of her, twining her fingers together. "He's here?"

"Not anymore. He left this realm three days ago."

Her eyes briefly flared, but soon returned to their usual dullness. "How intriguing. And Mr. Harrington saw my husband enter the portal?"

"So he says."

"And what else did he say?"

"Nothing."

"When did your husband go missing?" Quin asked.

"Just after Miss Moreau's previous visit, several days ago," she said.

Around the time the ghosts first appeared in Harborough. The timing fit together neatly.

"Is there anything else?" Mrs. Myer asked, once again glancing at the clock.

"Thank you for seeing us," I said. "I hope the next time we call upon you there is good news about your husband."

She *humphed.*

"Try not to worry," I added, simply to see her response.

"I never worry about him. If he insists on dabbling with forces he doesn't understand, he deserves whatever fate befalls him."

A more callous response I couldn't have imagined. She didn't even like her husband, let alone love him.

Quin and I left and walked back to Claridge's, where we

hired a hansom cab and drove to Samuel's house. The town-house was too large for a bachelor, and I suspected it had once belonged to his father and been a family home. The footman showed us into Samuel's study, where he received us warmly.

"I'm relieved that you could return to London so quickly," he said. "Has the ghost problem been fixed at Frakingham?"

"Not quite," I told him. "They've made themselves scarce. There's nothing to do in Harborough or Frakingham for the moment, so we thought we'd respond to your telegram personally."

"I'm glad. I think you need to speak to Faraday yourself, Cara. He might be more trusting of someone he knows."

"Did he contact you?" Quin asked.

"He did. After Cara left for Frakingham I decided to check his lodgings myself. I spoke to his landlady and looked around his rooms. It was as Myer described. Faraday had simply vanished, packing nothing, and not informing his landlady where he was going. I left my card and asked her to give it to him if he turned up. Yesterday, he came to visit me."

"Did he tell you where he'd been?" Quin asked.

"He said he couldn't remember."

"Couldn't remember!" I echoed. "Is he ill?"

"He looked in fair health to me."

Quin leaned forward and flattened his palms on the desk. "Did you ask him if he took the book from your lawyer?"

"I did and he claimed to know nothing about a book."

I blanched. "Nothing at all? But that's absurd. Why would he lie to your face like that?"

"Unless he's not lying," Quin said. "Myer may have hypnotized him into forgetting."

Samuel nodded. "That's what I think. I quizzed him on several events that happened before his disappearance, and he claimed to know nothing about any of them. He told me he couldn't recall much since arriving back in London from Melbourne."

"And you believe him?"

"He seemed genuine. Poor fellow was downright confused, actually. It's not the sort of thing that can be easily faked."

"Poor Nathaniel. Did you explain about hypnotism?"

Samuel shook his head. "I thought it best not to add to his troubles. Perhaps you could mention it and ask if he remembers Myer talking to him. He might feel more comfortable opening up to you than a stranger."

"I will. Speaking of Myer." I told him about Myer's disappearance and Harrington's ghost's claim that he'd seen him enter the portal.

Samuel's jaw hardened and his gaze turned flinty at the mention of the master. "You think he spoke the truth?"

"I have no reason to doubt him, particularly since Myer went missing at about the time the spirits emerged through the opened portal."

"But why would he tell you?"

"He told us he despises Myer. He does seem like the sort of fellow who would gladly cause problems for someone he disliked."

Samuel smoothed a finger over his lip in thought. "He's gone, you say? Returned to…Hell."

"I cannot be entirely certain, but I believe so."

He suddenly stood. "If you don't mind, I think I'll go and check on Charity, just to be sure."

"Of course." I caught his arm as we walked out of the study together. "Samuel, have you seen or heard from Lord Alwyn?"

"Nothing. It would seem he's still under my hypnosis."

"And now with Myer gone, there's no one to break it for

him." I stood on my toes and kissed his cheek. "Give Charity our warmest regards."

* * *

NATHANIEL FARADAY's rooms were located in a modest Chelsea house with a clean porch. Smoke billowed from a large chimney, and the smell of roasting meat wafted out to us when a white-haired woman opened the door and ushered us inside. Mrs. Curtin introduced herself as the owner of the establishment, then asked us to wait in the small sitting room at the front of the house while she fetched Nathaniel from his rooms upstairs.

He arrived a few short moments later, frowning. "Cara?" He spluttered a surprised laugh. "It *is* you!" He took my hand with great enthusiasm and squeezed a little too hard. "I'm so very pleased to see you again. Thank you for calling on me. Please, sit."

The landlady left the three of us and we sat. Nathaniel continued to grin at me for an uncomfortably long moment, until Quin cleared his throat. Nathaniel's smile slipped and he seemed to be waiting for something.

Another moment later he stretched out his hand to Quin. "Nathaniel Faraday. Pleased to meet you, sir."

"Actually, you've already met," I told him. "This is Quin St. Clair, a...friend."

Nathaniel's brows rose. I wasn't sure if he was questioning my use of the term friend, or whether he was surprised to learn they'd already met. "I'm sorry, I don't remember." He looked back at the door. "I can't remember much of the past few weeks. Ever since arriving back in London, as it happens." He rubbed his forehead. "It's damned frustrating."

"Samuel Gladstone told us you were a bit confused," I

said. "We're friends of his. He told me you'd come looking for him after he left his card here."

"Confused is one thing, but this is quite another. I...I can't seem to recall a single thing. Do you suppose I've been ill?"

"It's possible." I glanced at Quin.

Nathaniel's frown deepened. "What is it, Cara? I know you well enough to recognize when you're hiding something."

I smiled and my face heated. His warm familiarity surprised me. It had been missing from our recent encounters.

"She's not hiding something in order to keep secrets," Quin said evenly. "She's deciding how much you ought to be made aware of."

"Quin," I whispered.

But he ignored me and continued to glare at Nathaniel. Nathaniel put his hands up in surrender. "Of course. And I couldn't possibly know her as well as you do, could I, Mr. St. Clair. Tell me, how *do* you know Cara? I don't recall her mentioning your name in all the time we spent together on the S.S. Bombay."

Quin scowled and opened his mouth to say something.

"Our friendship began more recently," I said quickly. "Nathaniel, I think we need to tell you everything we know about your missing memories."

"Cara," Quin warned. "'Everything' may be too much."

"He may be able to help us."

"Or mislead us."

"Of course I'll help in any way I can," Nathaniel said. "If there's anything I can do for you, Cara, you need only ask. I hope you know that." His voice lowered a notch and I felt as if he were speaking only to me, focused entirely on me, despite Quin's presence. I wasn't sure what to make of it.

"The thing is, you may have been hypnotized," I said.

"Hypnotized!" He straightened, blinked, then laughed. "Cara, hypnosis is impossible."

Quin made a sound in the back of his throat that could have been a laugh or a grunt. He crossed his arms and arched a brow at me.

I turned my shoulder to him. "I know it's difficult to comprehend," I said to Nathaniel. "But hypnosis is very real, and we have reason to believe that Myer hypnotized you."

"Who's Myer?"

I sighed. This was going to take longer than I thought. I told him about Myer, his ability to hypnotize, and his interest in the paranormal.

"Paranormal?" Nathaniel smirked. His gaze flicked between us, and the smirk vanished. "Cara, what is all this about?"

"If you'll let her continue, you'll find out," Quin said pointedly.

Nathaniel apologized and rubbed his temples again.

"Myer had been searching for a particular book for some time," I went on. "It's a very old book that had been lost some time ago."

"Gladstone mentioned a book. He asked if I'd taken it. I had no idea what he was talking about. What was the subject matter?"

I flattened my palms across my skirts, bracing myself for more scoffing. "It contained some spells and information about the different realms that he wanted to study. He employed you to help him find it."

Nathaniel dragged his hand down his face. "Cara, I...I don't understand. You talk of spells and realms and hypnosis as if they're all real. I will admit that hypnosis may be possible, but the supernatural things..." He shook his head. The disappointed look in his eyes troubled me more than the fact he didn't believe me.

"It's real," I told him gently.

Quin leaned forward, the movement only small, but somehow he made it seem threatening. "If you knew Cara as well as you say you do, you would know she doesn't lie about such things."

"Not lie, no." Nathaniel pressed his lips together. "Cara, is it possible that you've been duped?"

Quin muttered something under his breath in French and appealed to the ceiling for patience.

"No, Nathaniel." I sighed. "Please, let me continue. This is what we think happened. You were hypnotized by Myer when you arrived back in London. He commissioned you to help him search for the book. Once he got his hands on it, he broke the hypnosis and wiped all memory of the last few weeks." I thought mentioning Myer's disappearance and the portal would be too much for him to take in, so I did not continue. Poor Nathaniel seemed at the end of his wits already.

"Why did he choose me? I don't know him and I doubt he would have known me. Why not hypnotize someone more knowledgeable? One of the historians at any of the universities perhaps, or even from the museum. My knowledge of antique books is limited, I'm afraid. My interest lies in the history of architecture."

"He wanted a *paranormal* historian." The problem with my statement struck me as soon as it was out of my mouth. I gasped. "You're not a paranormal historian, are you?"

"I think I'd be more accepting of realms and spells if I were." He grimaced. "Do you have another theory?"

I slumped back in the chair. "Quin? Can you think of an explanation? None of this is making sense."

Quin suddenly stood and strode to the window. He didn't stop to look out, but strode straight back again. He stopped in front of me, his eyes bright. "We're wrong. Myer didn't hypnotize Faraday. He was possessed."

CHAPTER 11

"Possessed!" Nathaniel blurted out. He alternated between laughing and staring at us with a straight face. "Cara, are you mad?"

"It would explain a lot," I said to Quin.

"You being mad?" he asked, amused.

I rolled my eyes. "Possession. When did you become aware again, Nathaniel?"

"Yesterday morning."

"Myer was already gone by then, so there's no way he could have broken a hypnosis." I wagged my finger at Nathaniel as a smile crept over my lips. More pieces of the puzzle suddenly fell into place. Quin was right. Nathaniel *must* have been possessed. "It explains why you didn't recognize me at King's Cross Station, that day. Even if you had been hypnotized, you still should have remembered me."

"We need to find that third medium," Quin said.

I nodded, thoughtful. "If we work out who possessed him, it could lead us to her. She must have orchestrated it."

"It's a place to begin, if nothing else."

"Whoever possessed you was clever," I said to Nathaniel.

"He played along remarkably well when we first met him in your body, at the Myers' house." I tried to think back to that day a few weeks ago. Nathaniel had called me Miss Moreau, not Cara, and only after Myer had mentioned me by name. He'd also seemed different to the Nathaniel Faraday I'd met on the ship. The man I'd wanted to get to know better had been charming and witty, self-deprecating and interesting. Later, he'd changed. His gazes unnerved me rather than thrilled me. Conversations were endured rather than savored. I'd wanted to get away from him.

"He might not even be male at all," I said.

Nathaniel made a choking sound and his face flushed.

"He was a man," Quin said darkly. "I'm sure of it."

"How can you be sure?"

"From the way he looked at you."

"Oh. I see." I cleared my throat. "He must have also been a paranormal historian. One that Myer knew."

"From the society."

"He did seem familiar with the library's layout and cataloguing system even though he claimed to have never been in it."

Quin and I smiled at one another, pleased with our progress. I'd forgotten Nathaniel was there until he coughed.

"Cara, I hope you'll forgive me, but…what you're implying…it's beyond belief. Please don't think that I'm disparaging you personally—"

"What are you doing then?" Quin asked idly. "Cara is telling the truth."

I glared at him until he looked away. What had gotten into him? "I know it's a lot to take in, Nathaniel. And I'm sorry we had to dump so much new and strange information on you all at once, but I'm afraid it's all true, and more besides."

"I'm not sure I can accept any of it without proof."

"I'm afraid I don't have any." I got up and crouched beside his chair. I placed a hand on his arm. "Your involvement ends here, anyhow. There's nothing more you can do to help us. If you like, you may chalk this up to a bad dream and forget we even had this conversation."

He smiled gently. "Thank you. But I don't want to forget any conversation I have with you. Even strange ones."

My face grew hot and my stomach did a little flip. Yet I was all too aware of Quin behind me. I could feel his intense gaze boring into my back and hear the deep breath he expelled.

I rose. "Thank you, Nathaniel. We must go. Once again, I'm very sorry."

He caught my hand. "You can't stay?"

I shook my head. Quin strode for the door, his steps long and purposeful. "Good day, Faraday," he tossed over his shoulder.

"What if I need to speak to you about any of this?" Nathaniel asked me.

"I'm staying at Claridge's for a few days."

He lifted my hand to his lips and kissed it without taking his gaze off mine.

Quin coughed so hard I thought he was choking. I withdrew my hand and followed him to the hansom waiting for us outside. We climbed into the cabin and gave orders to the driver to take us back to Claridges.

"Why were you so rude to him?" I asked as the coach jerked forward.

Quin stared out the window. "I was not."

"You were." I smiled. "I believe you're jealous."

A muscle in his throat throbbed and his lips tightened ever so slightly. I thought he wasn't going to answer me, until he eventually turned away from the window and met my gaze. "My apologies, Cara. But I didn't like the familiar way he spoke to you and touched you. Beaufort wouldn't have liked it."

"Jacob is not here. And I disagree. I think Nathaniel showed every politeness toward me. Jacob wouldn't have minded at all."

He turned back to the window. "I was trying to protect you."

"Oh, that's right, it's your *duty*. Well, Quin, I don't want you to be protective. I want—" I wanted his jealousy. I wanted him to fight for me. I wanted him to kiss me, and frighten away any potential suitors. I wanted him to claim me.

But what I wanted was impossible.

I stared out the opposite window, but saw none of the scenery through the tears pooling in my eyes. "You don't need to protect me from Nathaniel," I mumbled.

He didn't respond immediately, and I thought he hadn't heard me over the rumble of wheels. Then after a moment, he sighed. "I know. He is, mayhap, a better man than I first thought. If you were my kin, I wouldn't object to him courting you."

But he wasn't my kin, and I *wanted* him to object.

We traveled the remainder of the distance to the hotel in taut silence, but by the time we arrived, it had dissolved somewhat. I simply couldn't stay mad at Quin, and I hated not speaking to him. Besides, what we'd been arguing about wasn't really worth arguing over at all. I wouldn't waste the precious time we had together in petulant silence.

"I hope Jack has made reservations for dinner tonight," I said, taking his arm to walk inside. "Somewhere nice."

"Somewhere I'll need to restrain myself?"

I grinned, relieved he had decided to put our argument behind him too. "Somewhere there is so much food that you won't need to restrain yourself."

Jack hadn't made reservations because a dinner invitation arrived from the Culverts. He and Hannah greeted us in the small private parlor off the hotel foyer, where we relayed the events of our afternoon over glasses of sherry and brandy.

"It's fortuitous that we're going to see George tonight," I said when I'd finished speaking.

Jack raised both eyebrows. "Oh?" He and Hannah hadn't removed their gazes from me as I relayed the story, particularly when I expressed our thoughts on the possession of Nathaniel. "Why is that?"

"Because George is a well-known demonologist and it's possible that he knows most, if not all, of the paranormal scholars in London."

"The ghost is almost certainly a paranormal scholar," he said. "The London part is less certain."

"How did Mr. Faraday seem?" Hannah asked.

"Confused," I said.

"I'm not surprised. It would be an unsettling thing to learn that one has been possessed."

"Wait." Jack leaned forward. "You *told* him?"

"Of course," I said.

"Was that wise?"

"I thought he deserved to know the truth."

"And did he *believe* the truth?"

I was about to admit that Nathaniel had found it difficult without being presented with solid evidence, when Quin spoke. "Cara did the right thing. Faraday will come to see the truth in her words, if not soon, then one day. She's right. He deserved to know what happened to him."

Jack gave a small shrug. "It seems you two have decided to present a united front on the matter. I only hope that telling him doesn't come back to haunt you. Pardon the pun."

"Cara has good judgment of character," Hannah said,

setting her empty glass on the table beside her. "Now, we'd all better dress for dinner or we'll be late."

They walked ahead of us out of the parlor, giving me a chance to speak to Quin alone. "Do you believe what you said in there? That I was right to tell Nathaniel the truth?"

He put out his elbow for me, as Jack did for his wife. "You doubt yourself?"

I looped my arm through his, relishing the chance to be so close to him. "He seemed so disinclined to believe me."

"Most level-headed people need proof before they believe. I suspect he will spend some time searching for that proof, and when he inevitably finds it he'll change his stance. I hope to see him apologize to you, tail between his legs, before I go."

I smiled. "That is rather sweet of you, if somewhat vindictive."

"I have medieval views, remember?"

"Which you see through a lens that is becoming more and more modern with each day."

"I would take that as a compliment if I knew what a lens was."

* * *

GEORGE CULVERT DISMISSED his servants after they served dinner so that we could talk in private, but he did not touch a single thing on his plate while I recounted recent events. While his wife was horrified to hear about the disappearance of Myer and the book, George was fascinated, particularly on the topic of Nathaniel's possession.

Adelaide shuddered. "It's not a pleasant feeling when one realizes one has been possessed."

Hannah and Jack frowned at her, but I nodded in sympathy. I remembered when she'd been possessed many years earlier. I also remembered my role in that possession. I set my knife and fork down, my appetite suddenly disappearing, yet I couldn't tear my eyes from my food. Or, rather, I didn't want to meet anyone's gaze.

Quin, sitting beside me, closed his hand over mine beneath the table. He knew what I'd done, and he didn't blame me for it. It was the reassurance I needed to face the others again.

"We need to ask you some questions," I said to George. "The dead fellow who possessed Nathaniel must have been a paranormal expert. We hoped you might have known him."

"I may."

"George," his wife whispered. "Your food is going cold."

George picked up his knife and fork without taking his gaze off me. "He would have died recently, correct?"

"Not necessarily," I said. "He could have haunted this realm for years if he was unwilling to crossover."

"Well then, I can think of two—no, three—who died in the last ten years, all of them members of the Society for Supernatural Activity." He cut into his potato, but did not put any into his mouth. Adelaide gave him an exasperated glare that he didn't notice.

"Tell us what they were like," Quin said.

"Mathewson was elderly when he died, about nine years ago. Eighty or more, I think he was. Good friend of my father's too. He had an interesting collection of paranormal artifacts he'd brought back from his travels, as I recall. Most of them were bequeathed to the society."

"But what was he *like*?" Hannah asked.

"Yes, George," Adelaide added. "You haven't described the man, only the known facts."

George pushed his glasses up his nose. "I see. You're right. Well, he was somewhat stuffy, pompous. Thought I was an upstart with my modern ideas and suggestions. More than once he told Father that I ought to keep my foolish opinions to myself. He never addressed me directly. For all that, he liked to do things the right way. His research had method and order, and he never deviated from it."

"It wasn't him," Quin said. "Faraday's ghost wasn't pompous."

I agreed. "I have a theory about him. He tried to be flirtatious, but I suspect it wasn't something he was very good at. His attempts at flattery often fell flat. It was almost as if possessing Nathaniel boosted his confidence, but he couldn't quite pull off the air of a charming young bachelor."

"So perhaps he wasn't all that handsome in real life," Adelaide said, picking up her glass of wine. When everyone looked at her, she added, "Handsome men are aware of their good looks and have built up their confidence over many years because of it. Look at Samuel Gladstone and Jacob. Not to mention yourself, Jack."

"What about me?" George asked.

"You, Husband, are as charmingly oblivious to your handsomeness as you ever were."

He chuckled and began eating as if he'd just noticed his food for the first time.

"So we're looking for a dead member of the society who wasn't particularly handsome and was somewhat lacking in confidence around women," I said.

"He was also a coward," Quin added. "He kept his distance from me."

"To be fair, you were rather terrifying at times. As I recall, you were in a particularly bad mood at Hatchard's bookstore that day we went looking for the book of spells there."

His gaze slid to me. "You think I was terrifying that day?" He *humphed*. "I didn't even have my sword."

"Your sword is not what makes you scary."

He concentrated on his food just as George stopped

eating again. "It wasn't Bevan then. He was young and reasonably handsome, according to my mother who tried to, er, get his attention on more than one occasion. That leaves Holloway. Felix Holloway. He was around forty when he died, six months or so ago, of heart failure. He wasn't married and had few friends outside a small circle with similar interests in the paranormal. He was a short fellow and very round. I don't think anyone would call him handsome."

"What was he like?" I asked.

"I didn't know him well." He frowned and resumed slicing his food. "Although I didn't like the way he talked about you, my dear."

"Me?" Adelaide blinked at him. "Did I meet him?"

"He came here once to look at the library."

"I don't recall."

"You wouldn't. He was the sort of man one instantly forgets if one has only met him fleetingly."

"What did he say about Adelaide that you didn't like?" Hannah asked.

"He spoke about her as if she were a prized jewel that I'd been fortunate enough to win in a lottery. A pretty ornament, he called you, my dear. Not a word about your sweet nature or your kind heart. He only saw your face and figure, and your family connections of course."

Adelaide bestowed a soft smile on her husband who was now eating heartily. "Thank you, George."

He pushed his glasses up his nose and regarded her with a frown. "Whatever for?"

She pecked his cheek, still smiling. "Never mind."

"Felix Holloway it must be," I said, helping myself to more potatoes. "I'm convinced of it."

"So what's next?" Jack asked. "Will you tell Faraday?"

"Yes," I said, at the same time Quin said "No."

"There's no point," Quin told me. "How can Faraday help?"

"I wasn't expecting him to help. I just thought he ought to know."

He snatched up his wine glass. "It's not wise to involve him in everything."

"I agree," Jack said. "If he doesn't believe then it's too much of a risk."

"He might come to believe," Hannah said.

"In that case, wait until then. For now, we'll keep this information to ourselves. We'll inform Samuel, Charity, and everyone at Frakingham, of course."

"Emily and Jacob will want to know too," George said. "I'll write to them."

"So what will you do now?" Adelaide asked me.

"I'll summon the ghost of Mr. Holloway. Let's hope he hasn't crossed over yet."

* * *

GEORGE SENT ALL the servants away once we were settled in the drawing room with brandies and tea. He shut the door on the butler and signaled for me to begin.

I cleared my throat. "Mr. Holloway, are you there? Please come to us if you are still in the waiting area." A spirit could choose to come or not when summoned. It was entirely up to them, just as haunting was a matter of choice. I didn't hold out much hope that he would reveal himself, if indeed he hadn't already crossed over. He must know the sort of reception he'd get. Still, I had to try. "Mr. Holloway, we know what you did to Mr. Faraday and we only wish to talk to you about it. No harm will come to you, and you don't have to answer anything you don't wish to. Please," I added when nothing happened. "I'd like to see the real Felix Holloway since I grew to like him."

"That's devious," Hannah muttered with a sly grin.

Quin watched me with an amused gleam in his eyes as he stood by the mantelpiece. It would seem he harbored no jealousy toward *this* man.

"Would you now?" said the ghost that suddenly materialized in front of me. He was exactly as George described him—short and rotund with a web of tiny red lines across his florid nose and cheeks. What little hair he had was blond and too long, as if he wanted to preserve what was left of it. His eyes were an insipid blue, set close together beneath the smudge of his eyebrows. He must have thought all his good fortunes had come at once when he wound up possessing the handsome and charming Nathaniel.

"Somehow I doubt that you do want to know me better," he went on lazily. "Well?" He did a twirl, albeit an inelegant one that resembled a waddle more than a dance move. "Do you prefer this person to the other one?"

"Good evening, Mr. Holloway." My greeting made everyone sit up and glance around. Adelaide moved closer to her husband on the sofa, and he patted her hand for comfort. "No matter what you think, it *is* nice to see you again. You were quite an agreeable fellow when you weren't trying to flirt with me or hide something from us. That, sir, is the truth."

He chuckled. "Miss Moreau, are *you* trying to flirt with *me*? How the tables have turned. You must want something."

Quin picked up a book from the table and held it out, not far from the spot where the ghost glowed like a dim lamp. "Hold this, Holloway. We need to know where you are."

"The thug is still with you, I see." Holloway took the book. "Suppose you like his handsome face and musculature."

I didn't dare glance at Quin as I lied. "Not in the least. My tastes are a little more refined."

Holloway snorted. "Like Faraday, you mean? I admit that

part of the reason I chose him was because of his looks. I've admired his fine form for some time, and the way you ladies swoon whenever he speaks to you."

"I have never swooned, thank you."

"Not even for him?" He nodded at Quin.

"Especially not for him. Tell me, how did you know Nathaniel?"

"I really am a historian, albeit a paranormal one whereas he isn't. I wasn't always interested in the supernatural. I began my career in archaeology with a specialty in the Roman occupation of Britain, but later branched out when I discovered the existence of the supernatural. I liked to keep my hand in with my original subject, however. That's how I met Faraday. We both attended lectures at Cambridge before he went off to seek adventure overseas. Not that he remembers me, I suspect. Few people seem to. It was pure luck that I saw him at the British Museum the day after his return. That's where I died," he said upon my blank look. "I've been haunting the Elgin Marbles room. Remarkable pieces. Have you seen them?"

"Yes." I relayed what he'd told me to the others. "So you selected poor Nathaniel on purpose?"

"Poor Nathaniel?" he mimicked. "The man is blessed with the face of an angel. Don't pity him. When the opportunity to possess someone presented itself, I chose him because I wanted to see what it felt like to walk in his shoes for a while."

"And how did it feel?"

"Rather splendid, actually. It proves that people respond well to a handsome face. Women in particular. Do you know how many threw themselves at me?"

"I couldn't guess. Nor am I int—"

"Twenty-two." He nodded eagerly. "Twenty-two in a matter of a few weeks."

"Mr. Holloway, please, may we stay on track."

"Of course." He rocked back on his heels, clearly pleased with his efforts as a charming bachelor. "I was thrilled that my first choice of vessel worked. Even more pleased when I met you and discovered that you already liked me."

"Not *you*, Mr. Holloway."

His head jerked back as if I'd slapped him. His heavy jowls shook. "Careful, Miss Moreau. Don't offend me, or I'll disappear and you'll never find the answers to your questions."

The man was a toad, in appearance and manner. I hadn't disliked him when he possessed Nathaniel, but I did now.

"What's he saying?" Quin asked.

"Nothing significant as yet."

Holloway flipped the book open then snapped it shut again. Adelaide jumped. "What is it you want to know?" he asked.

"Who summoned you into Nathaniel's body?"

"I can't tell you that."

I bit back the retort that came to mind. Growing angry wouldn't get answers. "Please, Mr. Holloway, you must tell us."

"Why?"

"Because we can't have a medium going about summoning spirits into living bodies! It's a dangerous thing to do."

"Did I cause anyone harm?"

His retort took the wind out of my sails. "I…I'm not sure."

"I didn't."

"It can be argued that you harmed Nathaniel Faraday. He has to pick up the pieces of his life again after missing several weeks. Can you imagine his confusion?"

He snorted. "He's alive and well, isn't he?"

"And just because you didn't harm anyone, doesn't mean other spirits she summons won't do something horrid." The mysterious third medium had summoned Percy Harrington, and he had caused a great deal of harm to Charity and another girl. "She must be warned in case she isn't aware of the dangers."

He threw his head back and laughed so hard his belly shook. "Miss Moreau, let me assure you, the medium is experienced and is very aware of the consequences."

"Then why does she do it? Is she mad?"

He shrugged one shoulder.

"Or is she being coerced?"

"Coerced?"

"By Myer," I said, warming to my theory. "*He* requested the medium to summon you, didn't he? To help him with his research?"

He just smiled. It was maddening.

"Tell me why Myer chose you, Mr. Holloway. And why did you delay telling him the book was in Harborough? You allowed us to get to it first."

The smile broadened. "Miss Moreau, you're getting quite agitated. May I suggest that it's not good for your health to become so upset? Believe me, I ought to know. I became agitated at the museum when I saw they'd attributed my discovery of a Roman coin hoard to another archaeologist."

"I am not agitated," I said, breathing as steadily as possible to calm my thudding pulse. "Just answer my questions, if you please."

Quin came to stand beside me and rested a hand on my shoulder. "Cara?"

Holloway's eyes arrowed in on Quin's hand. His top lip curled and he screwed up his nose. "I ought to warn you about him, but I'm not sure you'll believe me."

I rubbed my temples where a headache bloomed. This conversation wasn't going at all as I'd planned. "That's not why I asked you here."

"But you want to know what I know." His sneer turned to a slick smile. "Don't you?"

Quin's hand was a comfort, yet I didn't dare look at him as I nodded. "Yes," I whispered.

"I asked them after I returned. The administrators." He circled Quin and I. Quin stiffened and kept his gaze on the book. His hand slid from my shoulder, down the back of my arm then let me go entirely.

I bit the inside of my lip. I ought to ask Holloway to stop, but I did not.

"Do you know what he did to get himself sent to Purgatory?"

I shook my head. "I can see that you're champing at the bit to tell me."

His smile broadened. He didn't bestow it on me, however, but on Quin. "You speak of worrying about the medium and the danger caused through the possession, yet there is a far more serious threat standing right beside you. You should be just as worried about your warrior, Miss Moreau. He's done something quite despicable. He murdered someone."

CHAPTER 12

olloway's accusation didn't have quite the effect on me that he probably wanted. I slowly breathed out my pent-up breath. "I'm sure there was more than one." Quin was, after all, a knight and a crusader.

Holloway turned that menacing smile on me. Quin's fingers pressed into my shoulder. "Killing in war is not murder and will be overlooked by the administrators," Holloway said. "Bringing justice to the deserving will also not cause a spirit to end up in the dark place after he crosses. Murdering an innocent man, however, will bring you to their attention."

"Is that it?" I asked, idly. "Or is there more to your story?"

"It's no story, Miss Moreau. It's completely true. I asked the administrators and they told me why people end up in Purgatory."

"But not him specifically?"

He lifted one shoulder. My question had Quin turning to face me. Did he know we were discussing him?

I cleared my throat. "If there's nothing else—"

"But there is," Holloway said. "I discovered why he needed

the book of spells. Or perhaps I should word it differently, seeing as you like to quibble over every point. I asked why a spirit in Purgatory would want the book of spells. I was told that it contained information that would enable him to get out."

"I know that," I snapped.

"Cara," Jack said gently, "could you relay what he's saying, please."

I put up my hand. "Soon."

Holloway shook his head and set the book down on the arm of the chair I'd been sitting on. He then went to stand directly in front of Quin, and puffed out his chest. He studied Quin's face, some distance above his own. "But did you know that he *wasn't* going to use it to crossover to the afterlife? He was going to use it to live again."

I snorted. "That's absurd."

"Is it?"

"It's not possible."

"How would *you* know, Miss Moreau? You're no expert."

"Cara," Quin said, "what is he saying?"

I looked at him and I suddenly realized that Holloway spoke the truth. Quin told me he wanted the book so he could move on, to get out of Purgatory. He hadn't said anything about living again. He hadn't lied exactly, but he had withheld the truth from me.

Oh, Quin. Why hadn't you told me?

"I must go," Holloway said. "And so must you. I believe you have your hands full with the escaped spirits."

I tore my gaze away from Quin. If I stared at him any longer, he would begin to suspect that I knew. A line had already formed between his brows. "You know about them?" I said to the ghost.

"Everyone in the waiting area knows. The administrators are quite worried, by the way. They're watching you closely. I suspect that's why there's a backlog of spirits waiting to be classified, myself included." He bowed. "Good evening, Miss Moreau. We won't meet again until your afterlife. As much as we haven't seen eye to eye very often, I don't wish you ill. I hope you have a long and fruitful life." His gaze slid to Quin. "Take my advice and choose Faraday. If he'll have you after finding out about your strange…talent. This one comes with too many burdens for a young, pretty thing like you to carry."

He was gone before I could say goodbye, but I said it anyway, for the benefit of my companions. I sat down again and gratefully slumped into the deep leather cushion with a sigh.

Quin crouched beside me. "Cara? Are you all right?" His voice was a soft purr that had me doubting Holloway's story. There was no way Quin killed someone in cold blood. He had a temper, but it was only ever directed at the deserving. If he'd killed an innocent, it must have been a mistake.

Adelaide refilled my teacup and handed it to me. "Drink this."

I took a long sip. The others waited as I did so. The room had gone very quiet and still as if none of them dared breathe. Once I set the cup down again, the tension broke and the questions flowed.

"What did he say?" Jack asked.

"Did he mention who summoned him?" said George.

Hannah put up her hands for silence. "One at a time. Allow her a moment to gather herself."

"Thank you, Hannah," I said. "Holloway told me very little. We still don't know who the medium is. He refused to say."

"Blast," George muttered. "Well that was bloody pointless."

"Not necessarily." I took another sip of the warm, sweet liquid to fortify my nerves. All I could think about was Quin using the book to get out of Purgatory and live—live!—and me having stopped him by withholding the book.

Oh God. What had I done?

I clutched the china tighter and stared down at the tea until I felt I could face them and go on. I did not look at Quin. He was right beside me, his presence a distraction for all of my senses. It was like he was a magnet, sucking me in, scrambling my brain.

I took another sip. "He told me very little, but I noticed something peculiar as he was speaking. He never referred to the medium's gender. Not once did he say her or she. Is it possible that mediums can be male?"

George shook his head. "Not according to historic sources. They're very clear on the matter."

"How many historic sources are there?" Jack asked.

"Very few."

"That doesn't sound definitive. We should entertain the possibility that mediums can also be male."

"Then wouldn't Louis be a medium?" I asked. "My father and nephews too?"

Nobody had an answer. Quin didn't seem to be listening at all, despite continuing to stare at me. It was unnerving. How could I hide my thoughts from him when his gaze burrowed into me like that?

"I'll consult the texts again," George said with enthusiasm. "I may have missed a reference the first time."

"It's getting late," Hannah said. "We should go."

Adelaide rang the bell for the butler. When he arrived, she asked him to have their coach fetched from the mews. We rose and our hosts saw us to the front door themselves. After saying our goodbyes, we climbed into the coach and took off for Claridge's. It didn't take Jack long before he asked the question I knew he'd been dying to ask for some time.

"Why haven't you told us everything Holloway said to you, Cara?"

"I relayed the necessary part of the conversation," I told him. "The rest was private."

"What could he possibly say that was private?"

"Jack," Hannah warned. She didn't need to say anything else. Her husband let the matter drop, but not before giving Quin, sitting beside me, a meaningful look.

Quin remained ominously silent for the rest of the journey.

* * *

I'D BEEN WAITING for the light knock on my bedroom door for an hour, but when it came, my heart still jumped. "Who is it?"

"You need ask?" came the quiet, deep rumble of Quin's voice.

The hairs on the back of my neck rose. I adjusted the shawl over my shoulders and opened the door. The sight of him dressed in nothing but shirt and trousers never failed to take my breath away, and this time was no exception. However, where his expression was usually one of assured-ness, tonight doubt and worry tugged at his mouth.

I opened the door wider to let him in, but he hesitated. "It's not like we haven't been alone in a room together before," I said.

"There is usually a chaperone." He glanced up and down the hallway then slipped inside and closed the door.

"Sylvia hardly qualified to be called a chaperone, considering she slept like a log."

The corner of his mouth flicked up in a smile before quickly settling again. He had not taken his eyes off me since entering, and I was beginning to be unnerved by the intensity in them.

"This is just like old times," I said, padding across the floor to the bed. I tucked my feet up beneath me, adjusting my nightgown to cover them, and indicated he should sit on the armchair by the fireplace. "I missed these quiet conversations the most when you were gone." I hadn't meant to sound so wistful, nor did I want to reduce myself to tears, but they burned the backs of my eyes nevertheless.

His steps slowed for a moment before he continued to stride to the armchair. "I missed them too. I missed many things about this realm."

"Like the food?"

He smiled as he eased himself into the chair, but it didn't last long. "The food. And you."

I smoothed the creases out of my nightgown with long sweeps of my hand over my legs.

"Forgive me," he said quickly. "I shouldn't…" He got to his feet and headed back to the door. "I shouldn't have come."

"Quin, wait." I leapt off the bed, getting tangled in my nightgown in my haste. I landed on my hands and knees on the rug. My cheeks flamed with humiliation, but at least my pathetic fall made Quin stay.

He gently grasped my arms and helped me to my feet. His thumbs stroked me through the light linen, warming my skin. "Are you hurt?"

"No. Thank you."

He let me go and picked up my shawl. He settled it around my shoulders, his knuckles grazing the underside of my jaw. I lifted my gaze to his face, only to see him staring back at me with such intensity that my entire body flushed with tingles in response. He removed his hands, but I caught them in my own. I drew one to my lips and kissed the knuckles. He opened his other hand and cupped my face.

An ache so deep and endless welled inside me. I felt like my heart was full of tears, barely contained behind a wall that was slowly, slowly crumbling.

There were so many things I needed to say to Quin, yet this was not a time for talking. It was a time for touching, holding. Kissing.

He gently tilted my face up and I let go of his hands to grasp his head and draw him closer. He didn't resist or hesitate. Suddenly the gap was closed and our bodies, lips, hands joined. I was slammed up against him, my arms around him, and his around me, holding me as if he were afraid I would escape.

But I would not. Could not. There was nowhere else I wanted to be. The frenzied kiss destroyed thoughts of all else. There was only Quin and me, the kiss, and the heat rising within me, evaporating my tears. I felt like I was drowning in it, being sucked under the surface by a whirlpool, and into a beautiful, wonderful abyss that I never wanted to leave.

I dug my hands through his hair, holding him as tightly in place as he held me. I didn't want the kiss to end. Didn't want to awake from the beautiful dream and face cold, brutal reality. I wanted to remain in Quin's arms forever. It felt wonderful, and so very right. Yet it wasn't enough.

I fumbled with the buttons on his shirt and managed to undo the top two. I slipped my hand through the gap and felt the smooth skin of his shoulder and the small scar nestled there. It reminded me of the new scars on his back, and thinking of them made me lose the rhythm of the kiss.

It was Quin who pulled away, however. He let me go and stepped back.

No! I swallowed the cry before it escaped and made a strange gurgling sound instead. I blinked at him and tried to catch my breath and regain my wits, but it was terribly hard to wade through the fog of desire still shrouding me.

He seemed to be doing the same. His chest rose and fell with his deep breathing, and his eyelids drooped like heavy shutters. His fists closed at his sides as if he were stopping himself from taking me again in his arms. Despite his rigid stance, he looked thoroughly kissed, with his messy hair and swollen lips.

I wondered if I looked the same. My body was certainly tightly coiled as I tried to hold myself together. If I released my emotions, the floodgates would open and there was no telling when they would close again. Such a hysterical response would get us nowhere.

A small frown creased his brow and he looked away, down at his feet. "Cara, I...I'm sorry." He opened his fists and rubbed the back of his neck. "I shouldn't have done that."

"*You* didn't. *We* did."

He shifted his stance.

"I don't regret it, Quin."

He didn't respond.

"Indeed, I liked it. Very much. I think you did too."

He lifted his gaze to mine and pinned me to the spot. "What we like and want doesn't matter. We're making it harder for ourselves by allowing affection and desire to rule us."

"You make it sound like we have a choice."

He swallowed heavily. Then he spun round and strode for the door. I raced past him and flattened myself against it.

"You're not leaving yet," I told him.

"I have to, otherwise..." He heaved a sigh and dragged his hand through his hair. "I may be dead, but I am still a man and this body is very much alive in this realm. There is only so much kissing that will satisfy me. And I won't ruin you, Cara."

Oh. Right. "Then we won't kiss anymore. We'll talk only. Isn't that why you came here? Or were you planning on kissing me the entire time?"

He looked offended. "I am still a gentleman, my death

notwithstanding. Very well, we'll talk. But you must stop looking so enticing."

"Oh."

He pointed to the bed. "Sit there and wrap the blanket around yourself."

I did as told, then went to push my hair off my face.

"Do not play with your hair," he ordered as he sat down again. "Do not lick your lips, touch your face or allow that blanket to slip. And absolutely no blinking your big eyes in that manner you have."

I bit back my smile. "That is quite a lot of rules."

"All of them necessary. Now we can talk. What did Holloway say to you?"

Any lingering desire shriveled up. I pulled the blanket closer around my shoulders, but it didn't offer as much comfort as Quin's arms. "He told me something about you, as it happens."

He didn't look surprised and nodded at me to go on.

"You let me believe that you were leaving Purgatory to move onto your afterlife. Holloway told me that's not true. You wanted the book to learn how to leave Purgatory and come here."

His gaze shifted away from me to the wall behind the bed. So it was the truth.

"You wanted to live again." My voice became a whisper as the tears clogged my throat. "Why didn't you tell me?"

"Would it have made a difference?"

"Yes! I would have given you the book."

He shook his head. "I'm not so sure of that."

"How could you know what was in my mind?" I spat. "Of course I would have given you the book. I want you here, Quin. I want you with me." To my horror, I couldn't hold the tears back anymore. I pressed my forehead against my drawn up knees and let my tears soak the blanket.

"Cara," came Quin's gentle voice. "It pains me to see you cry."

Then hold me. Comfort me.

But he did not.

I finally lifted my head and wiped my cheeks. Quin still sat in the chair, both hands gripping the arms, the fingers making deep dents in the leather. "You did the right thing in keeping the book from me," he said. "I think you know it and would do so again."

"But why didn't you tell me at the time that you could have come back here, alive? I should have had all the facts."

"I didn't tell you because I didn't want your decision to be any more difficult than it was. And I didn't want you to have any regrets."

"Too late for that."

"Any *more* regrets."

I had to concede that he had a point. If I'd known what I was preventing him from doing, I would have been wracked with guilt at sending him back to Purgatory without the book.

"Bringing back a man condemned to Purgatory is unwise," he went on. "You knew that at the time, and I've come to realize it too. I committed a grave sin, Cara. It sickens me to admit it, but I must acknowledge it. I deserve my punishment. The administrators would never allow me to leave that realm until they themselves release me. It would not have gone well for me if I'd used the incantation in the book." He rose to go. "You saved me, Cara. Thank you."

I swallowed heavily. "Sit down. We haven't finished."

He hesitated then sat. "Did Holloway say something else?"

"He told me you killed someone. An innocent. That's why you're in Purgatory. Is that the grave sin you speak of?"

His nostrils flared and he drew in a long, deep breath. Then he nodded. "Is that all?" he said.

"He knew no other details. I hoped you would give them to me."

He shook his head. "I once told you that I didn't want you to think ill of me. Nothing has changed. Telling you what I did…it will only make you hate me."

"Why not let me decide that?" I snapped.

"Cara, don't. Please." He stood and headed for the door. I scooted off the bed and got there before him. This time I didn't fall over and there was no affection between us. "I want answers, and I will not let you leave without giving them to me."

He sighed. "Ask me anything. Anything at all. But not that."

My mind went blank. I could think of no other questions. That one was burned into my brain, excluding all others.

"I'll tell you about my wife, my home, the king. I'll tell you how I came to respect my enemies and hate killing them. And that I loved my mother and didn't care for my father. I will tell you how I miss my brother." His voice caught. He cleared his throat. "Ask me, Cara. Ask me *something*. Just not that."

I folded my arms over my chest, holding myself together. "Very well. You once told me that the rules didn't apply to you and that's why you're still a warrior in Purgatory and haven't moved on. *Why* don't the rules apply to you?"

He blinked rapidly and I suspected my question caught him by surprise. "My death was brought about by…unusual circumstances."

"Supernatural ones," I finished for him. "You said so last time."

"My death should not have occurred if the administrators had been doing their job efficiently." He held up his hands when I went to ask another question. "No more, Cara. Please. My death is linked closely to my reason for being in Purgatory. To tell you about one will mean telling you about the other." He reached out and stroked his thumb from the corner of my eye down my cheek. "Your good opinion means everything to me. I won't shatter it, even if it means you pester me with questions from now until eternity." He gave me a sad smile and dropped his hand.

I tightened my arms, hugging myself harder. I began to tremble uncontrollably, yet I wasn't cold.

"Good night, Cara."

"Don't go," I whispered.

"I have to, *mon coeur*."

"I'm not moving."

Light from the burning candles danced in his eyes, or perhaps it was mischief. "I thought you might say that." He picked me up by my elbows and lifted me out of the way.

"Unfair!"

He set me down, kissed my forehead, and disappeared out the door.

* * *

WE RECEIVED a telegram from Tommy early the next morning. *They're back* it read.

Quin and I packed immediately. Jack wanted to return with us, but Hannah convinced him to stay to conclude his business in London and take her to the Gilbert and Sullivan opera at the Savoy as planned. I suspected she was more interested in keeping him safe than seeing *The Yeomen of the Guard*. The injury he'd suffered at the Tudor house had given her quite a fright. Jack reluctantly agreed, but only after giving us a lecture about being vigilant and sending for him if needed.

The train departed that morning, and Quin and I spent most of the journey in awkward silence. We both either gazed out the window or pretended to sleep. I didn't mention the kiss, since there was nothing more to say. Nor did I pester him with questions about his death or Purgatory. While the silence was awkward, it wasn't tense, and toward the end of the journey I fell asleep.

I awoke when the train slowed for the approach to Harborough Station. Quin watched me from beneath half-lowered lids, but quickly looked away. It was rather amusing, and very satisfying, to see the skin above his collar flush pink. I was still smiling when he held out his hand to assist me onto the platform.

"Cara! Quin!" Sylvia pushed past a passenger, waving her hands. Tommy trailed behind. They'd received our telegram, then. "Thank goodness you were able to come so promptly. We'll take you there immediately. Quin, do you have your sword?" She eyed his luggage.

"Always." Quin greeted Tommy with a nod. "Is everyone safe?"

"Everyone at the house," Tommy said. "The villagers, however, are anxious. The ghosts returned yesterday and made a nuisance of themselves overnight. Weeks and his men have had their hands full." He stepped in close and lowered his voice so the nearby passengers couldn't hear. "The inspector reported seeing odd things. Objects flung about with nobody throwing them. Women having their skirts lifted, and worse."

"You must stop them." Sylvia grasped my hand. "We'll talk more in the coach."

Quin carried our bags and followed behind with Tommy. Fray helped him load the luggage onto the back of the coach after Quin removed his sword, wrapped in a cloth. He slid it under the seat in the cabin, and Sylvia ordered Fray to take us to the police station.

"The spirits are causing trouble there?" I asked.

"They're tearing the place apart," Tommy said.

"What do the inspector and his constables think of that?"

"They're confused, naturally, and at their wits end."

"How will we explain this away?" Sylvia squeezed the bridge of her nose. "We can't blame it on wild dogs this time."

"We'll think of something," I assured her. "But first, we must remove the spirits."

Quin pulled out the sword and rested it on his lap. He unwrapped the cloth from around it. The sunlight glinted off the blade. "Did you bring the knife, Dawson?"

Tommy pulled back his cuff, revealing the point of Jack's dagger. We'd left it with him to keep them safe in case the spirits came back while we were gone.

I held out my hand for it, but he shook his head. "I'll hold onto it, if you don't mind. You direct us."

"Tommy, don't," Sylvia said, huffily. "Haven't you suffered enough?"

Tommy gave her a flat, grim smile. "I can't sit in here while Cara risks her life. You know that, Sylvia. Doing so would injure me more."

"I know." She kissed his cheek. "I know."

He laid the knife in his lap and placed his hand over hers. They remained like that the rest of the way to the station. It would seem their relationship had made progress in our absence. I was pleased for them, but curious if Langley knew and if so, what his reaction had been.

We arrived at the police station only a few short minutes later. The coach hadn't even stopped before Weeks emerged through the gap where a door had once stood. I breathed a sigh of relief at seeing him alive and unharmed. The door, however, had not fared so well. One half of it rested up against the wall, and the other half lay on the pavement.

"Evacuate your men," Quin said as he opened the coach

door and jumped out. "We'll take care of the matter from here."

"It stopped," Weeks called out. He eyed Quin's sword, his nose twitching. "The storm ended some minutes ago."

"Storm?" I asked, stepping out of the coach.

"It was the oddest thing, Miss Moreau. Things flew around the room as if a whirlwind had taken hold of them. A tempest, Constable Jeffries called it. I don't mind admitting that I prayed like a nun. Hid like one too, under the desk. Jeffries tried to catch the typewriter as it hurtled toward him, but he didn't duck fast enough. He's all right now. He's inside, cleaning up the mess left behind when the wind died down."

"So there was a wind?" I asked, keeping my voice bland.

"Must have been." Weeks screwed up his face and squinted through the doorway. "How else would things fly around like that?"

"Of course." I glanced at the others. "There's no other explanation."

Quin peered through the doorway, but did not enter. I heard the tinkle of glass being swept up and the scraping of furniture across the wooden floor.

"It only began after the door came off," Weeks went on. "Splintered in two it did. It was about then that the wind came, I think. Can't recall exactly, but that's how it must have happened. Anything that wasn't too heavy got flung about." He squinted up at the sky. "All looks calm out here now, I see. Very odd that it only affected the station."

"I've heard of strange phenomena like that," Sylvia assured him, patting his arm. "Intense storms that are all wind and no rain. They only ever occur in small areas. Very small, very local areas."

Quin returned to the coach and held the door open. "Come to us at the house if there's any more trouble. Fray!" he called up to the driver. "Drive slowly through the village."

"Wait." Weeks rested his hand on the door handle, stopping it from closing. "The problem at the Tudor house continues."

I exchanged a glance with Sylvia. "The wild dogs, you mean?"

"Is it?" he asked suspiciously. "Or is it gypsies?"

"I'm sure it's dogs," Tommy said.

"You see, I was speaking with Dr. Gowan only yesterday, and he said he didn't treat scratches on your cousin, Miss Langley. It was a knife wound."

"I'm sure he's mistaken," Sylvia muttered.

"The good doctor knows the difference between cuts caused by claws and those left by knives. My guess is that Mr. Langley didn't want the gypsies to get into trouble."

"That must be it," I said. "He's got a good heart and the gypsies aren't all bad. He wouldn't want to see them blamed for the problems the village is currently having."

"Seems a strong coincidence to me that they've turned up at the old Tudor house right when we've had extra reports of trouble in the village. I don't like coincidence, Miss Moreau. In my experience, there's always a better explanation."

"Have you paid the house a visit?" Quin asked.

"Not yet. Been too busy here, and now this storm." He tugged on the lapels of his jacket. "But I can tell you, the villagers aren't quite so busy. There've been rumblings of forming a mob and going up there to...talk to the gypsies."

Sylvia sat forward. "You must talk them out of it, Inspector! It's far too dangerous."

"Good of you to be so concerned, Miss Langley, but I can't stop an entire village. There's too many of 'em."

"Have you even tried?"

He looked away. It would seem he didn't *want* to talk them out of it. "Best be on your way now." He slapped the coach door. "Give Mr. Langley my regards."

The coach drove off. I watched Weeks through the window until we rounded the corner, then I scanned the streets and buildings for signs of ghostly trouble. It was all quiet.

"Fool," Tommy muttered.

I nodded gravely. "If a mob forms and goes to the Tudor house, they'll be set upon by Redbeard and the others."

"They'll be armed," Quin said. "I'm sure they can protect themselves."

"But they'll be at a disadvantage, unable to see their attackers, only their weapons."

"Not to mention they'll discover the truth about ghosts." Sylvia clasped her hands in her lap and appealed to me. "After all our attempts to keep the paranormal a secret, it will finally come out in such a dramatic manner. They'll think us mad. They'll think themselves mad!"

"Let's not worry about that until it happens," I told her. "Besides, people tend to explain away what they don't understand. You saw how Weeks responded to the damage done to his station."

Sylvia peered out the window too. "I'm surprised he fell for the storm story. Relieved but surprised."

"People believe what they want to believe."

"His mind is closed to the possibility of the paranormal," Tommy said. "It's beyond not only his comprehension, but his imagination too."

"Something to be thankful for," Sylvia muttered. "Let's hope the rest of the village lacks imagination too."

We drove down the main streets and some smaller ones too, but saw nothing untoward. Tommy asked Fray to go past the Tudor house next, but it too was empty.

"They've gone again," I announced after a walk-through of the old house.

"Damnation," Tommy muttered. "I'd hoped to resolve this once and for all."

I hazarded a glance at Quin, but he sat stoically, his back straight, the sword on his lap. If he wanted the ghostly problem resolved too, he gave no sign. I, however, sighed heavily. I didn't want it to end just yet. When the ghosts left, Quin would return to Purgatory and I might never see him again.

We continued on to Frakingham. The now familiar sight of the house seemed more inviting than ever with the reflection of the afternoon sun setting the dozens of windows ablaze.

One of the lower ones suddenly exploded, sending glass shattering onto the garden bed. Sylvia screamed.

"Bloody hell!" Tommy stared, wide-eyed, as Mrs. Moore's frightened face peered out of the glassless window. "I think we've found the spirits."

CHAPTER 13

ommy, Quin and I raced up the front steps and
pushed open the door. Sylvia gasped at the mess
that greeted us. The wall mirror had been smashed and the
hat stand overturned. Hats and umbrellas were strewn across
the floor. The front of the long case clock stood ajar, and the
mechanisms had been pulled out like the guts of a slaugh-
tered pig. It was perhaps fortunate that the entrance hall was
sparsely furnished. I hated to think what the library must
look like, or Langley's laboratory.

"Cara?" Quin asked.

"Empty," I said.

A crash came from directly above us. The chandelier
swayed and plaster dust snowed down onto the floor tiles.

"Uncle!" Sylvia moved off, but I caught her arm and
Tommy blocked her way. "I have to see if he's all right!"

"Keep your voice down," I hissed. "We have to take them
by surprise."

"But Uncle August and Bollard may be in trouble."

"And how will we take them by surprise?" Tommy asked,

looking up at the ceiling again. "They probably saw us arrive."

Quin set off up the stairs, forcing the rest of us to follow or be left behind. I picked up my skirts and ran to catch up so that I could be alongside him. "Stay behind me," he warned.

"I won't be able to see them if I'm behind you."

We crept as silently as possible to the first floor landing. I caught Quin's arm, halting him, and nodded in the direction of a ghost with his back to us, gazing out the window.

Quin sliced his sword through the empty air and raised his brows at me. I shook my head and put out my hand for the sword. Reluctantly, he gave it to me. I crept up behind the ghost and chopped the blade lengthways through his body. He half turned, gasped, and tried to say something, but couldn't speak. I reached into the chest cavity and pulled out his soul. Fear flickered in his eyes before I crushed the black mass.

I handed the sword back to Quin. Sylvia turned her face into Tommy's shoulder.

Another crash nearby made me jump and Sylvia mutter a cry that she covered with her hand. Quin headed toward it, but I held him back. I needed a weapon. It didn't need to be an otherworldly blade, just something to defend myself and drive them toward Quin and Tommy if possible.

I removed the flowers from the vase on the table beneath the window and grabbed the candelabra off another. I handed the latter to Sylvia, but she shook her head and eyed it dubiously. I shoved it at her chest, forcing her to take it.

Then I headed into the parlor alongside Quin. The spirits spotted us immediately. They set down the chair they were about to hurl through the window and eyed Quin's sword.

"There's three," I said. "By the window."

"Blimey!" said one of the ghosts who then disappeared.

"Now there're two." I doubted the third had decided to

return to the afterlife. More likely he'd gone to warn the others. I could still hear them throughout the house, crashing about, breaking things. I prayed that Bollard, Langley and the servants were unharmed.

The two remaining spirits sneered and picked up broken chair legs. They didn't bother with Tommy, but descended on Quin. Perhaps they should have gone for the semi-crippled target, because Quin slayed them easily, felling both with a single stroke. Tommy removed the soul of one while Quin accounted for the other.

The dust hadn't even reached the floor when more spirits appeared.

"Four!" I shouted. "Two on your left, Quin, one by the fireplace and another...here." I threw the contents of the vase over the spirit nearest me. I wasn't sure if water was like solid objects or would pass right through him. It wet him thoroughly, however, and he spluttered and blinked as any live person would do.

"Bitch!" he shouted at me, wiping his eyes.

I smashed the vase into his face, sending him reeling backward. "Tommy! There!" I pointed at the soggy ghost, but Tommy had already spotted him—or rather, he'd noticed the indentation the ghost's body made in the armchair he'd fallen into. He ended the spirit's existence a mere moment later.

Sylvia raised the candelabra, ready to strike. "Any more, Cara?"

I looked around. Quin had destroyed one and was fighting another two who used the wooden chair legs as weapons, but with far more finesse than the first ghosts. He dispensed with one nevertheless, but another two popped into existence. They'd picked up books before I could alert anyone, and flung them at us.

Tommy and I moved out of the way in time, but one

struck Sylvia in the hip. She hissed in pain and rubbed her hip. Tommy barged forward, the knife raised high.

"Show yourselves, cowards," he growled.

The spirits merely laughed and moved away. There was no point telling Tommy where they'd gone. The ghosts would simply move aside or leave altogether. He would waste energy in trying to strike them. Energy he didn't have.

It happened to Quin too. They'd gotten smarter. Every time he disarmed a ghost, the spirit would disappear, only to reappear elsewhere, usually behind him. It was hopeless. We couldn't go on like this. The only saving grace was that the spirits weren't armed with knives, only table and chair legs, or the odd book or ornament.

Until Redbeard appeared, sword in hand, flanked by another ghost.

"Quin! Behind you!"

He spun and slashed in a swift, deadly move that saw Redbeard's companion fall and Redbeard himself step back in shock. He watched, a stunned expression on his face, as Quin removed the fellow's soul and his dust joined that of the others on the carpet.

"Give up," I ordered Redbeard. "This is madness. Your friends are being destroyed."

The shutters came down over Redbeard's eyes, narrowing them to slits. "They're not my friends," he snarled. "And I'm not going back there. I'm not going anywhere." He slashed wildly at Quin, only to be driven back to the doorway.

Quin went after him, but Redbeard managed to slip out to the corridor. The *clank* of metal on metal moved further away, but I hesitated to follow. I couldn't leave Tommy and Sylvia alone. If the spirits had any sense at all, they would realize that I was gone and their opponents were vulnerable. It would only need an attack from behind to cause terribly injury.

Out in the corridor, Redbeard roared in frustration. "You there!" he shouted. "Attack from the side. And you, behind him!"

Bloody hell. "Quin, behind you! Tommy, Sylvia, with me. *Now!*"

I ran out of the parlor and fortunately they followed. I heard Tommy grunt in pain and Sylvia gasp, but a thud and another grunt, this time from one of the ghosts, told me they were working together.

"Syl, against the wall," Tommy directed her.

I glanced over my shoulder to see them both with their backs to the wall, lashing out at chair legs and ornaments.

Quin, on the other hand, was fighting off four ghosts alone. I slammed the vase into the back of one's head. It didn't fell him as it would a live man, but it did get his attention. He bared his teeth at me and flexed his hand around his knife handle.

"Cara!" Tommy shouted.

I glanced at him as he dropped the knife to the floor and kicked it toward me.

"Look out!" Sylvia screamed.

I spun back round. The ghost descended on me, poised to strike. I put up the vase and his blade clanged against the porcelain, knocking me off balance. I fell heavily on my side and had no time to recover before the ghost came at me again. I thrust the vase up once more to shield my face, but he kicked it out of my grip. I was unarmed and vulnerable.

He stood over me. "Got you now, bitch."

Sylvia screamed, but there was nothing she or Tommy could do, occupied as they were with their own battle. Quin was also busy with Redbeard and two other spirits, but Sylvia's scream had him turning toward me.

He swore in French and ran toward my ghost. Redbeard's blade nicked his shoulder and another sliced across his arm as Quin shoved the spirit out of the way. Blood oozed out of the wounds, but he didn't seem to notice. He was too intent on the blade descending rapidly toward me.

With the knife mere inches from my chest, Quin cut through the ghost. The spirit screamed and dropped his weapon beside Jack's blade. He fell to his knees, but Quin had no time to pull out the soul.

"Behind you!" I shouted.

He turned and parried Redbeard's swiftly descending sword. I reached into the injured ghost and removed his soul. His dust covered my skirts, bunched up at my knees. I kicked his knife across the floor to Tommy who used it on the ghost attacking him, then I picked up the otherworldly blade and stabbed the same ghost in the back.

He grasped at the wound and opened his mouth to cry out in shock or pain. But it was too late. A moment later, he became a pile of dust. His companion soon followed suit, and another spirit who'd hung back near the parlor door disappeared altogether. Hopefully he'd decided Hell was better than nothingness.

"Give me Jack's knife," Tommy said, holding out his hand. "Quin needs help."

I could have helped him myself, but I handed it to Tommy. Sylvia clasped me tightly as we watched him take one of the spirits by surprise, stabbing him in the back just as I had done with his attacker. Tommy still had dust from the ghost's soul on his hands when Redbeard turned toward him.

I called out to warn him, but Tommy had already spotted the sword coming at him and dodged it. Redbeard disappeared then reappeared behind Quin.

"Duck!" I screamed.

Both Tommy and Quin flattened themselves to the floor. Quin struck out as he did so, cutting the second spirit's ankles. He fell over, dropping his weapon. Quin went to stab him where he assumed his chest to be, but missed. The ghost scooted across the floor on his rear, out of reach.

"Get up!" Redbeard shouted at him.

The ghost shook his head rapidly. "I never wanted this." Then he vanished.

"Coward!"

Quin and Tommy stood back-to-back, ready to strike in any direction. But no attack came. With a roar of fury, Redbeard threw the sword at them then disappeared himself. Quin parried the blade away.

"They're gone." I listened, but could hear no voices or other sounds from the house. "All of them."

"Uncle!" Sylvia called. "Uncle, where are you?"

She went to race off, but I caught her hand. "Wait. We must remain together. There might be an ambush."

We headed up the stairs to Langley's rooms, but neither heard nor saw any more spirits. We finally reached the topmost floor and pushed open the door to the laboratory. To my surprise and relief, it had been left untouched. The books were all in place on the shelves and the scientific equipment seemed to be as it should be, unbroken on the benches. The room smelled of burnt metal and I spotted the culprit at the furthermost bench. I went to turn off the gas burner, but Quin beat me to it. He studied the contraption with a frown. I leaned across him and switched it off.

There was no sign of Langley or Bollard, except for the wheelchair positioned near the bench. Langley must have been studying the reaction of the liquid in the dish over the burner when the ghosts struck. The liquid was now a black, sticky mass that didn't look like it would come off the dish very easily.

"Uncle?" Sylvia called out.

"Here." The muffled voice came from the cupboard behind us. Quin opened the door and Bollard stepped out,

Langley in his arms. Langley's hair was mussed and Bollard's face drawn tight, but they appeared unharmed.

Sylvia flung her arms around them both and emitted a small sob. He patted her back then directed Bollard to set him down in his wheelchair.

"Are you both all right?" Sylvia asked, wiping her damp cheeks. "We were so worried."

"We're unharmed," Langley said. "We hid in there as soon as we heard the ruckus." He surveyed his collection of books, notes, equipment, and the dozens upon dozens of jars and containers. "Thank God they didn't come in here."

"They would have found plenty to occupy themselves," I said with a wry smile at Bollard. "We are very glad you're all right."

"And the rest of the house?" Langley asked.

"It'll require some tidying up. We'd best check on the servants."

Quin headed toward the door before I'd even finished speaking. I picked up my skirts and followed him.

"We gave most of them the afternoon off," Tommy called after us. "There was little to do here with you all gone. Glad we did."

"But I saw the housekeeper at the window."

"Poor Mrs. Moore," Sylvia said on a sigh. "She has no family in the village and nowhere to go on her days off. She's rather a fixture here now." She pressed her hand into Bollard's and he smiled back at her.

"Go and help find her," Langley said to his niece. "When you do, have her bring up some tea."

I rolled my eyes at his uncaring manner, but only Bollard saw. He gave me a flat smile then winked.

"This is why I didn't want more servants than necessary," I heard Langley mutter before I left the room. "They see too much."

We found Mrs. Moore cowering under the kitchen table, wringing her apron. She would not come out until I coaxed her with the promise of a cup of hot chocolate. Tommy set about making it over the stove while Sylvia and I sat Mrs. Moore down.

"Flying about the room, they were," she muttered. "Candles and books just floating through the air. I've never seen such a thing. Have you, Miss Langley?"

Sylvia took Mrs. Moore's trembling hands in her own. "Are any of the maids or footmen in the house?"

Mrs. Moore shook her head then looked around the kitchen. "Lucky this room was spared or Cook would have been very displeased. She likes her things to be kept in order. Do you want me to serve your dinner, Miss Langley? Cook left it all for me to do."

"It's quite all right, thank you. It's not yet dinnertime, and perhaps we can serve ourselves tonight. Indeed, we might even eat in here at this very table. Won't that be an adventure?"

Mrs. Moore gave a horrified gasp. "Miss Langley! I must protest. I admit that the house is in something of disarray, but that doesn't mean we lower our standards. On the contrary, we must raise them! It's only through maintaining the natural order of things around here that the world will return to normal. Indeed, it would be a comfort to me to see everything going on as it should."

Sylvia patted her hand. "Very well. So, uh, what do you think caused the objects to fly around the house?"

"Why, Mr. Langley's experiments of course."

"Pardon?"

I pressed my lips together to smother my smile.

"He's always doing strange things up there. Doesn't like me going in and touching anything. I've suspected for some time that what he did was magic."

"It's science, Mrs. Moore," I assured her.

Sylvia stared hard at me and shook her head. "Magic, science…it's all the same, isn't it?"

The housekeeper nodded. "That it is, Miss Langley."

Quin had finished checking the larder, scullery and other service rooms and was heading for the main door that led back out to the hallway.

"Where are you going?" I called after him.

"To inspect the rest of the house."

"Not without me." I caught up to him at the entrance to the service stairs. "Quin, slow down. I need to look out for more spirits. There might still be an ambush."

We searched the house from attic to basement and every cupboard and nook in between. Frakingham was indeed free of ghosts.

"I wonder if they've gone back to the Tudor house." I eyed Quin closely as we climbed the basement stairs. While he moved easily enough, his jacket and shirt were torn, and blood darkened the fabric.

"We'll go there tomorrow," he said.

"Yes, of course. You'll need time to recover. Tomorrow it is."

He stopped at the top of the stairs and rounded on me. "Very amusing. We'll go tomorrow so *you* can rest tonight."

Enough mockery and teasing. The time for that was over. I fingered the rent in his sleeve near his shoulder. "You must allow me to tend to your wounds."

"I don't think that's wise."

"I don't care about wise."

His eyes turned smoky. "I do."

"And anyway, I do think it's wise to inspect them. They could fester if they're not properly tended to."

"There's no need. I'll be leaving soon. My wounds will

heal when I return to…" He blinked slowly. "When I am back where I belong."

My fingers twisted in the fabric of his sleeve. He winced, but made no sound as I brushed against the wound underneath. "You don't belong there," I hissed.

"The administrators would argue otherwise. As would I."

"You are not a bad person, Quin." Tears clogged my throat and burned my eyes. It was difficult to rein in my emotions and give voice to my thoughts, but I battled to control them until I felt I could speak without bursting into tears. "Whatever you did…there must have been a reason. I know you don't want to tell me, and I respect your decision, even if I don't understand it. But without knowing what you did, you must allow me to defend you."

"Cara." He laid his hand over mine and gently untangled my fingers from his sleeve. I hadn't realized I'd bunched the material into my fist. He pressed my hand to his heart, where a steady, pounding rhythm made me ache for him. "I am returning soon, whether you like it or not. That is fact."

My fingers curled under, but I did not pull away.

"As soon as the ghosts are gone, I will leave this realm again. We removed many here today, and I suspect many more will leave voluntarily now. There must be some remaining or I would have already been called back. It won't be long now. You must prepare yourself for another farewell —as I am trying to do." He kissed the top of my head then removed my hand from his chest and let it go. "So please, there will be no more touching, even if it is only to check my wounds." The corner of his mouth lifted. "We both know how that always ends, and it only makes it harder when I have to go."

He walked away, leaving me standing at the top of the basement stairs alone, hot tears rolling down my cheeks.

* * *

"YOU SHOULD REST," Sylvia said, hand on hip. She wagged a statuette of the Goddess Diana at me. "You may be needed in the village tonight."

"I can't rest." I lifted the box filled with broken pieces of china off the dining table and turned to go.

Quin blocked my exit. He grasped the box and tried to pull it out of my hands. I didn't let go. "Sylvia's right. Rest, Cara."

I glared at him. "I thought you wanted to wait until tomorrow to patrol the village."

"I do, but we may need to go tonight."

I tugged on the box, but his grip was too tight. He lifted one brow in a challenge. I tugged harder, but still he did not let go. "You're the one who ought to be resting," I said. "*I'm* not injured."

"A few scratches do not require me to lie down like a woman."

"Ha!"

He pulled the box out of my grip while I was too busy thinking up a retort. He grinned triumphantly.

"You did that on purpose," I said.

He gave me an innocent look. "Did what?"

"Implied that my gender is weak in order to rile and distract me."

"You must be mistaken, Cara. I would never call women weak. Some of the strongest people I have known, in my lifetime and my afterlife, have been women." He strode out of the dining room, box in hand, with his head held high.

I thrust both hands on hips and thought about chasing after him and taking the box back, but in truth, it had been heavy and it would just be petty of me.

"You two make me laugh," Sylvia said, a twinkle in her eyes. "It's a shame you can never be together."

"Sylvia," Tommy gently admonished her.

She shrugged at him. "It's not as if she doesn't know that already."

I sighed. "Excuse me. I think I need some fresh air. I'll be down by the lake if anyone needs me."

The sun had set and there was little moonlight, but I knew the way to the lake. I skirted the abbey ruins, preferring not to be reminded of all the gruesome and frightening things that had happened there thanks to the portal.

The portal. Instead of going onto the lake, I stopped at the outermost ruined wall after all, and studied the haphazard shadowy formations of the fallen stones where the portal was located. So many strange things had come through it, including the ghosts of Redbeard and his black-hearted friends. They were not meant to be here—just like Quin.

I swept my skirts aside and sat on the wall. Thoughts raced through my mind like windswept leaves. I tried to grasp them, but as I reined one in, another would escape and flitter just out of reach. I took a deep breath and stopped trying. Then I began at the beginning.

The portal had brought beings from other realms to this one, and taken people from here to…elsewhere. Some of them were alive, but others were dead. Redbeard was dead. Quin was dead. So if Redbeard could remain here, couldn't Quin too?

Surely it couldn't be that simple, or Quin *would* stay. Myer must have done something before opening the portal—or perhaps during. He must have spoken another spell that caused Redbeard and the other souls to be brought here. If I could find out what he did, perhaps I could figure out a way to make it bring souls from Purgatory, and Quin could stay.

I heard Quin's footsteps. The rhythm of his tread was as

familiar to me as my own. He sat beside me on the wall, but we didn't touch. Nevertheless, I was all too aware of him, and my heart skipped inside my chest at being so close, shielded from prying eyes by darkness.

"It won't work," he said.

"What won't?"

"Opening the portal and keeping me here indefinitely."

I turned to him. "How did you know what I was thinking?"

"Because we think alike, and I've already considered it."

"Oh." I looked back at the ruins again. It was deceptively peaceful with the long grass swishing gently against the stones. If there were any signs of the blood that had been spilled and the horrors that had brought fear and violence, they couldn't be seen in the dark. "It's hard to believe that the abbey stood proudly here for many years before its destruction, yet it was built after your death. So long ago."

We sat in comfortable silence, but the weight of time hung heavily around us, and the weight of Quin's current situation even heavier.

"You've adapted to this world well," I added, "considering your advanced age."

He laughed softly. "I had a good teacher."

"I'm not sure I've taught you much at all. Except how to eat with a knife and fork." I smiled, but did not look at him. "Why won't it work, Quin? You could come back, like Redbeard. It wouldn't be a perfect situation, but at least we could be together."

"And watch you grow old and die while I never changed? That's no life, Cara. That's torture. I'd rather be sent to Hell than exist alongside you and not *with* you."

I sighed. He was right, and it was wrong of me to suggest it. Quin couldn't live as a ghost with only me seeing him. It wasn't a life, it was a sentence and he'd grow to hate it.

"Besides, they wouldn't let me go so easily," he said.

"The administrators? Why not?"

"Because they want to keep me in Purgatory, and going against their wishes would anger them. They'd send another warrior here to bring me back."

I sighed again. "We can't have that." I tried to sound light when all I felt was heavy. "One of you is quite enough. My modern feminine sensibilities couldn't cope with another caveman attitude."

He chuckled. "I don't know how men in caves are meant to behave, but I'm sure they would like you despite your sharp tongue and mind. They would learn the hard way not to cross you."

I nudged his arm. "Come on. We ought to go back inside and help."

"Or rest." He yawned. "I'm feeling somewhat sleepy."

I nudged him again and laughed, but it died at the sound of hooves pounding on the gravel drive. I squinted at the line of trees, but couldn't make out the rider, only his lantern, swinging wildly back and forth as he held it high. Quin leapt off the wall and helped me down. He held my hand as we ran toward the house where the rider had come to a stop.

"It's Constable Jeffries," I said as he dismounted near the lamps blazing at the foot of the steps.

Sylvia and Tommy emerged from the house as we approached. "Constable Jeffries," she said. "What happened?"

The policemen removed his hat and gave her a nod of greeting. "Excuse the late hour, Miss Langley, but the inspector asked me to fetch Mr. St. Clair."

"Is it the village?" she asked. "Are there…storms again?"

"Nothing like that, miss, although there's reports of noises coming from the Tudor house."

Sylvia and Tommy looked over the constable's head to Quin and me. "We'll head there now," I said.

"No, Miss Moreau, that's not why I'm here. Inspector Weeks said I was to fetch you and ask you to come to St. Paul's, opposite the green."

"Why? What's happened there?"

"The mob's gathered inside. The villagers are getting riled up over the disturbances the gypsies have been causing. The inspector thinks you might be able to disperse them before they march on the Tudor house. He's worried someone'll get hurt, but he thinks Mr. St. Clair might have some sway with them seeing as he's not from around here. He says you've got a presence that commands respect," he told Quin.

"We'll go immediately," I said, grasping Quin's hand tighter.

But he didn't move. A muscle pulsed in his jaw as he turned dark eyes onto me. And then I realized why he hesitated.

He couldn't enter the church without falling violently ill.

CHAPTER 14

"Only speak if they're not too riled," Quin said, casting a wary eye at the arched door of the church. A voice could be heard beyond it, but I couldn't make out his words. "If you think they won't listen to you, then say nothing. Don't anger them further." Quin wrapped his fingers around my arms and gave me his full attention. His face was pinched, his jaw rigid.

"I'll gauge the situation first." We'd been through this already in the coach, twice, but he still seemed to think it needed repeating. "I'll have Tommy with me."

"That may not be a good thing." He shrugged an apology to Tommy who stood nearby, waiting for Quin to finish his lecture. He hadn't asked why Quin couldn't go into the church, but I suspected he was going to when this was over. By then, it probably wouldn't matter if we told him Quin was from Purgatory. He would be gone. "As Jeffries said, somebody who is not from around here may fare better with the mob." I opened my mouth to speak, but he cut me off. "No, you are *not* going in alone, Cara."

"I'll be fine, Quin. I'll leave if they become too rowdy."

He flexed his fingers but did not let me go. Just then, a cheer erupted inside the church. I pulled away and headed up the steps with Tommy. I glanced back at Quin. He paced alongside the coach, his expression unreadable in the deep shadows cast by the streetlamps.

Tommy pushed open the door and we went through to the nave. Thick candles burned in the sconces along the walls, throwing their flickering light into the cavernous church. Standing straight ahead, in front of the altar, was the stocky figure of the Harborough mayor. "Butterworth!"

A few people at the back of the crowd turned to look at me. They nodded in greeting before once more listening to what their mayor was saying.

"His wife's over there, near the choir pews." Tommy nodded at the imposing figure of Mrs. Butterworth, standing with a straight back at the side of the church. Every once in a while her husband would look at her and she mouthed something or nodded at him to go on. It was as if he was acting as her mouthpiece in front of the villagers. "Are there any ghosts?"

"Not that I can see." It was possible that spirits from Hell could not enter the church. If Quin couldn't, it made sense that they couldn't either. "Weeks is near Mrs. Butterworth and there are another two constables, as well as Jeffries, stationed near the other exits."

Tommy shook his head. "They won't be able to stop anyone."

"Nor can we. This crowd won't listen to reason."

There must have been fifty people standing or sitting, mostly men. Some held clubs or pieces of wood, others appeared unarmed. They shuffled restlessly, and their cheers and calls for justice punctured Butterworth's speech.

"They cannot be allowed to come here and disrupt our village!" His voice boomed through the church, reverberating off the stone walls. He may not be able to think as quickly as his wife, but the man had a strong presence that the people responded to. "We are good, law-abiding *English* citizens and we have a *right* to not be afraid in our streets."

"Hear, hear!" shouted several voices from the audience.

"We have a right not to be afraid in our homes!"

"Amen!"

"We have a right not to be afraid in our beds at night!"

A chorus of voices called out their agreement.

"These heathens must be stopped!" Butterworth slammed his fist into his palm to shouts of approval from the crowd. "They must be brought to justice! We have had enough of fear and lawlessness. We want to take back our beautiful, *peaceful* village."

"Aye!"

"Hear, hear!"

"If the police won't act, we must!"

The mob's roar drowned out Weeks as he joined Butterworth. He seemed to be calling for calm, but his words were lost in the din.

Then suddenly the crowd surged toward Tommy and I. He hustled me out of the way, wincing as his bad arm was jostled by a large man pushing past.

"Are you all right?" I asked him.

He nodded. "We have to get outside, but I'm not sure what we can do to calm them."

He was right. The mob wouldn't listen to us. They only wanted to hear the message of violence and revenge. What could we say, anyway? Telling them that there were no gypsies, or that ghosts couldn't be brought to justice, would only see us ignored or laughed out of the village. It was an impossible situation.

"We must hope that they'll calm down when they see

nobody at the Tudor house," Tommy said, his fingers firmly gripping my elbow.

"And that Redbeard and his friends will behave." It seemed like a futile hope. Redbeard wasn't the behaving type.

We were about to join the mob as it streamed through the doors, but my other elbow was gripped hard. Weeks's narrow features appeared before me.

"Where's your foreign friend?" he hissed.

"Outside," I said, as Tommy got swallowed up by the mass of people leaving the church. I spotted his head above the crowd, and waved him on. He couldn't fight his way back toward me and I was safe enough with Weeks.

"He better try something to calm them, or the old house will be destroyed, and everyone in it."

"Inspector, what is it you expect Quin to say or do?"

He merely shrugged, then he too moved off into the flow, where he was dragged along in the mob's wake.

I waited until the tail end of the crowd had passed me, and I joined the Butterworths as they left. Mrs. Butterworth arched an imperial eyebrow at me, swept her gaze up and down my length, then sniffed and strode ahead. She had never liked me, despite my connection to the earl of Preston through Emily. Although she managed to be polite in social situations, she rarely addressed me directly, and never remembered my name. Like the gypsies, I was un-English in her eyes. I saw no point in wasting energy trying to change an attitude that ran as deep as bedrock and was just as immovable.

Her husband wasn't quite so rude. At least he deigned to address me. "What are you doing here, Miss Moreau?"

"Constable Jeffries fetched us. We hoped to stop you from advancing on the Tudor house."

"Why would you do that?" He seemed genuinely puzzled. "Those gypsies must be stopped."

"And if people are harmed in the process?"

"They'll deserve it."

"I'm not only referring to the...gypsies. Some of the villagers might come to harm too."

"I'm sure they all agree that the risk is necessary. We are defending our homes and families after all."

"What will you do if there's no one there?"

"We shall see, won't we?" He smiled. "Besides, the gypsies *must* be at the Tudor house. There have been many reports of noises coming from inside." He touched my shoulder, very close to the bare skin at my neck. "Go back to Frakingham, Miss Moreau. I wouldn't like to see that pretty face of yours get a mark on it." He brushed his thumb along my neck above my collar and I was about to jerk away when I was wrenched backward by a firm arm around my waist.

I slammed into Quin's chest and glanced up at him. His pale face shone with a fever and his eyes were glassy, but he still managed to instill enough menace in his glare to send Butterworth scurrying away to join his wife.

I felt the tension ease from Quin's body as he slumped against me. He shuddered, but did not let me go as I faced him fully. I pushed his damp hair out of his eyes and felt his skin. It was hot.

"You shouldn't be in here," I told him.

"I couldn't see you." He closed his eyes and drew in a shuddery breath that didn't seem deep enough to fill his chest. "Dawson...was alone."

I looped my arm around his back and tucked myself into his side, propping him up as best I could. "We have to get you out."

He doubled over, gripping his stomach. The grinding of his teeth was louder than the noise of the mob outside.

"Quin! Please, you have to help me. I can't get you out alone."

But instead of walking, he collapsed to his knees, dragging me down with him.

"Go," he rasped. "Leave me."

"No!" I tried to haul him up, but he wouldn't budge. He turned away from me and was violently sick on the floor.

"Cara?" Tommy called from the doorway. His gaze slid to Quin. "Jesus Christ. What's wrong with him?"

"He needs fresh air. Help me get him outside."

"What's wrong with the air in here?"

He didn't seem to require an answer as he placed his good arm around Quin. Between us, we managed to get him to stand, and he stumbled out through the door and down the front steps. He collapsed against the coach, rocking it, and sucked in deep breaths.

I rested my palm against his back, but it wasn't enough. I needed to be closer, to listen to his breathing and feel the response of his body. I pressed my cheek between his shoulder blades and closed my eyes against the sting of tears.

After a few more moments and deep breaths, he finally stopped shuddering and straightened. The muscles beneath my cheek tensed. Reluctantly, I drew away.

"Better?" I asked as he turned.

His face was still somewhat pale, but the fever had disappeared from his eyes and his skin no longer looked waxy. He inclined his head in a nod. "You should have left me."

"No. *You* should not have come inside."

"Dawson came out without you." As if that explained his stupidly dangerous action!

I planted my hand on my hip and was about to admonish him when Tommy reached between us and opened the coach door. "Stop bickering. The mob moved off."

He was right. The crowd had disappeared. Only the faint echo of their shouted accusations could be heard. We climbed into the coach, but Fray had to drive out of the village via a different route and circle it in order to avoid the road clogged by the crowd. We parked the coach some distance away from the Tudor house, where Fray and the horses would be safe, and walked to the property. We carried no lamp, but my eyes quickly grew accustomed to the darkness. We did not go in through the front gate, but remained at the side, where part of the fence had fallen over and overgrown shrubs provided coverage.

"We don't have much time," Quin said. The mob hadn't arrived, but they would soon.

"We'll take them by surprise," Tommy suggested.

I agreed. "It's our best advantage."

"It's our *only* advantage."

"No." Quin withdrew his sword. "This is our advantage. And Cara."

I gave him a weak smile, but he didn't return it. Perhaps he hadn't seen it in the poor light, or perhaps he wasn't in a smiling mood. He'd been quiet ever since we'd dragged him out of the church. I suspected his masculine pride had suffered a blow after I'd seen him weakened. Or perhaps, like me, he knew the moment for goodbyes was almost upon us.

Tommy pulled Jack's knife from his inside jacket pocket and handed it to me. "Take this."

"No." Quin pushed Tommy's hand away. "Her reach isn't long. She won't get close enough to use it if they're armed."

"But she must defend herself."

Quin tugged on a half-buried fence paling and pulled it free of the soil and weeds. He handed it to me. "Let's go before the mob arrive."

"Wait." I collected a handful of soil and filled my skirt pocket. "Ready."

Quin stopped me with a hand to my shoulder. "Cara..." He sighed and lowered his head.

"I know," I said heavily, fighting back tears. At Tommy's

quizzical look, I added, "Quin will be leaving as soon as we've sent the ghosts back."

Tommy gave me a sympathetic smile then turned it on Quin. "Thank you, St. Clair. You're welcome to come back any time."

"I would gladly return." The unspoken 'if I could' hung like a dense raincloud in the air. He tightened his hold on my shoulder, then let me go and led us across the fallen fence into the tangle of shrubs that formed the side garden.

I joined him and we crept up to the house. He nodded at the nearest window, and I crouched in front of it and peered through, while Quin and Tommy flattened themselves against the wall out of view.

Moonlight lit up the room beyond. It was large and contained a fireplace with a blackened mantel surrounding it, and scorched walls and beams. There was no furniture or ghosts. I moved onto the next window then the next. Each time, I shook my head to signal that the room was empty. A few more windows later, we reached the kitchen. It had probably once been separate from the main house, but was now connected by a wooden structure that appeared to be caving in on itself.

I heard them before I saw them. I put my finger to my lips and crept closer to the window. It was too high for me to look through. To save money in a time when glass was a luxury item, the Tudor-era builder had made the windows small in the service area and high to catch the light.

I signaled to Quin and he crouched near me. He set down his sword and linked his hands together. I placed my foot in the cradle and he lifted me until I could see over the sill. A single lamp hung on a hook beside the door, providing enough light to see all eight ghosts, including Redbeard, lounging on or around the table. They appeared to be armed with knives.

I rested my hand on Quin's head and he lowered me. I held up eight fingers then drew a map of the room in the earth with a stick, placing dots where the ghosts sat.

Quin picked up his sword and slowly, gently tried the nearest door. He shook his head. Locked. We headed back to the front and found it unlocked. We crept through the house using instinct and what little light the moon gave, to find our way to the rear. We tested the floorboards as we went, and I winced every time a loose one groaned. But no ghosts appeared.

Redbeard's raucous laughter drifted through the warren of rooms to us. I paused, worried he'd seen or heard us. But there was no sign of him, and the voices still sounded like they came from the kitchen at the back of the house.

We continued and reached the flagstone area that marked the beginning of the makeshift corridor linking the main house to the kitchen. Quin and I went first, his sword poised to strike, his left arm stretched protectively in front of me.

There did not appear to be a door to the kitchen—it must have come off at some point—and I could clearly hear the ghosts' conversation. They were discussing the delights of a particular woman from the village, and the 'fools' who were on their way. So they knew about the mob. That explained why each either held a knife or had one in front of them on the table.

Quin didn't wait for me to throw soil over the spirits. He charged straight in and struck the nearest ghost straight through the chest. My drawing had been accurate enough that he'd not needed to see him. The spirit's soul was crushed before the others had time to gasp.

They gathered up their weapons and fell back, away from Quin. My map was no longer of any use, but at least he and Tommy knew their positions from the physical objects they held.

"Come on, lassie." Redbeard beckoned me with a crook of his finger. "Come and tug on old Red's beard. I'll show ye' what a real man can do." He grasped his crotch, and his friends snickered.

"You don't belong here," I told them. "We're going to make sure you don't remain. Choose now—an afterlife or nothing."

A young spirit near the back of the group dropped his weapon. "I'm going." He disappeared.

"Coward!" Redbeard shouted into the ether. "Anyone else want to follow that pathetic boy?"

All the other ghosts remained. Redbeard nodded with satisfaction then focused on Quin.

Quin charged first. I winced at the clash of metal on metal, so loud in the small room. "Get back, Cara!" he shouted at me.

I did not. Tommy and I worked together. I threw a handful of soil at the faces of the two nearest ghosts. They cursed me and rubbed their eyes. Tommy sliced through the chest of one then another straight away. I pulled out their souls and squeezed them to dust. Then I threw their dust at another two.

One spluttered and blinked rapidly, but the other emitted a high-pitched wail and dropped his weapon. He frantically tried to brush the dust from his face and shook out his hair.

"Get 'im off! Get 'im off of me!" He wiped his dirty nose then vanished altogether, amid another hysterical wail.

The disappearance of yet another spirit didn't affect Redbeard this time. He was too busy with Quin, and the two remaining ghosts joined him. Three to one. They were odds I didn't like, particularly as Redbeard blinked out then reappeared.

"Behind you!" I shouted.

Quin spun and swiped. His sword glanced off Redbeard's shoulder. The ghost hissed in pain, but didn't pause as he returned the strike. Quin dodged it easily enough, but had to be careful of the others' knives.

"Back to back with Quin," I told Tommy. "It's the only way."

Tommy moved to join him, striking one of the spirits straight through the heart. I removed the soul for him and threw the dust at another advancing toward me. Where had he come from? Blinded by the remnants of his friend, he didn't see the fence paling coming. I struck the hand that held a knife, knocking it away. It slid across the floor until it hit the lip of the hearth.

Two more ghosts suddenly appeared. One picked up the knife, while his companion removed a copper saucepan from a hook above the fireplace. They came at me together.

I lashed out with the paling, striking the one with the knife in the shoulder. He lost his balance and stumbled to the side, but the other kept coming. He raised the saucepan with both hands and brought it down.

Quin's sword flew through the air and pierced the ghost. The spirit screamed, but soon lost his essence and his voice as the power of the blade took hold. He dropped the saucepan and it broke into two pieces on the floor. I removed the sword and reached into the cavity. His soul came out easily.

I brushed its dust off my hand and turned on the other ghost who'd recovered his balance. I sliced the sword cleanly through his body. He dropped his knife, blinked rapidly, then disappeared before I could remove his soul. Hopefully he'd taken himself back to Hell.

A grunt behind me had me turning quickly. Quin was unarmed, his sleeve a bloody mess. He dodged strike after strike from Redbeard, while Tommy fought off the only other remaining ghost.

Quin put out his hand and I threw the sword. He caught

it, dodged another of Redbeard's blows, and re-engaged him in battle.

I came up behind Tommy's opponent and slammed the paling into his head. While it didn't injure him, he did make him lose his balance, giving Tommy the opening he needed. He sliced him through the chest with Jack's knife and I removed the soul.

Tommy and I wasted no time. We rounded on Quin and Redbeard. Realizing he was alone against three of us, Redbeard stepped back.

"Weaklings," he spat at his missing friends.

"Return," I ordered.

"Never!"

He charged at Quin. It was an erratic, foolish move that propelled him headlong at Quin's sword. But instead of striking Redbeard's body, Quin stepped aside and let the ghost stumble past. Shelves nailed to the wall collapsed, sending plates, bowls and clay pots smashing onto the floor.

"What are you doing?" Tommy cried. "You could have ended this."

I stared at Quin. He glanced at me then away, flexing his fingers around the sword hilt. My heart dropped into my stomach. Quin hadn't ended it because that would mean he had to return to Purgatory. Redbeard was the only remaining spirit. We both knew it.

"You can stay," I said to Redbeard before I lost my nerve.

"Cara." Tommy's sharp tone left no doubt what he thought of that. Quin did not meet my gaze or speak.

"You can stay if you promise not to do any harm."

"No, Cara." Tommy's voice held sympathy, but a warning too. "He's dangerous. You can't trust his promise. Nor can you make that judgment."

The muscles in Quin's jaw bunched and relaxed, bunched and relaxed, as he continued to avoid my gaze. He did not move to strike, but the fingers holding the sword became white. He seemed to be warring with himself.

As was I. Hot tears pricked my eyes. I wanted to close them and curl up into a ball, but I didn't trust Redbeard. I had to watch his every move. Tommy was right—someone with a soul evil enough to be sent to Hell could not be trusted. We had to destroy him.

Redbeard got to his feet, laughing. He pointed his sword at Quin. "Turned into a fool by a wench."

"Quin."

My plea had him finally looking at me. The shine in his eyes did not hide the torment and ache. "I'm sorry, Cara."

I tightened my grip on the fence paling and nodded. "As am I. Goodbye."

His nostrils flared. He raised his sword to engage Redbeard as Tommy prepared to strike from behind. Redbeard was trapped and he knew it. He disappeared.

"Christ!" Tommy swore. He did not glare at us, but I knew he blamed us for letting the ghost escape.

I blamed myself. "Do you think he's returned to Hell?"

Quin shook his head. "He won't go back there. I can see the fear in his eyes whenever it's mentioned."

"Then where—"

Redbeard reappeared in the doorway. He was armed, not with a sword, but a pistol. He aimed it at Quin.

And fired.

CHAPTER 15

"Quin!" My scream was barely out of my mouth as Quin dove to the side. He crashed into a washing tub, splintering the rotten wood. Blood poured from his thigh.

I ran to him.

"No!" he shouted. "Stay there!"

I stopped and followed his gaze to where Redbeard still stood, the pistol aimed at Quin. He cocked it and grinned.

"Got you now," the ghost sneered.

Tommy raised his arm to throw the knife, but Redbeard swiveled and pointed the pistol at him. Tommy ducked behind the table, thank God, Jack's knife still in his hand.

Redbeard chuckled. "I have them now, miss. So what will *you* do? Or should I see the reaction when I aim this at you."

Hell. Quin would put his body in front of mine if Redbeard carried out his threat. I couldn't allow that. He might already be dead, but his body was essentially alive in this realm. I wasn't sure what would happen if it were to die again. He might never come back.

Quin heard them before I did. He cocked his head ever so

slightly, listening. The shouts of the mob erupted in the distance, moving quickly toward us. Redbeard heard them too.

"So they come," he said with a firm nod. "What will they do when they discover your bodies here and no gypsies?" He twisted and aimed the gun at me.

Quin leapt up.

"Bloody hell, there's no one holding it!" The voice at the high window had Redbeard, Tommy and me turning to see who spied on us.

But not Quin. He shot past me and grabbed the gun in Redbeard's hand. They wrestled with it and a shot went off. The bullet dug into the brick chimney.

Tommy and I had the same idea at the same time. I grabbed Quin's sword and we both ran to help him. I thrust the sword into one side of Redbeard and Tommy sliced his knife into the other side at chest height.

Redbeard's mouth opened in a silent scream. His eyes filled with pain. He tried to grasp at my hand as I reached into the hole we'd gouged out of him, but he passed right through me. I clasped his soul in my palm and did not hesitate as I crushed it.

Quin placed his hand at the back of my neck. It was then that I realized he'd angled himself so that the onlooker at the window couldn't see the soul or its dust. I blinked up at him, wanting to say so many things, but saying none of them. We'd already said our goodbyes, there was no point repeating myself.

I offered him his sword and he took it, closing his hand over mine. My heart beat out a rapid rhythm in my throat. His thumb massaged my neck. His gaze locked with mine. It was filled with longing and an earnestness that I felt deep in my bones.

He kissed the top of my head, but it was light, airy, as if he was already disappearing. I let go of the sword and closed my eyes, committing the feel of his lips against my skin to memory.

"Through there!" came a shout from the main part of the house.

Quin pulled away and I opened my eyes. He was faint, his body little more than an outline. Tommy stared at him, unblinking. He saw what I saw.

"Get out of here," Quin ordered, his voice painfully thin. "Too dangerous." He seemed to be having trouble speaking. His lips drew together and his jaw clenched hard.

Tommy pocketed Jack's knife and grabbed me by the hand. He led me to the rear door, letting me go long enough to unlatch it. He guided me through, but I refused to go any further than the threshold without Quin. He'd followed us, but he was as indistinct as an artist's preliminary sketch.

"Quin," I sobbed. I reached for his hand, but my fingers passed right through him. He was in ghost form. Soon, he would be gone altogether.

Yet he fought to stay. I could see it in the way he closed his fists at his sides, and the determined set of his jaw. He held my gaze and I covered my mouth to smother my sobs.

His lips moved, forming my name, but no sound came out. He grimaced in frustration. Then his jaw clenched harder.

But he could not fight forever.

"Go, Quin," I murmured.

The sounds of the mob crashing through the house behind us drew his attention. He glanced over his shoulder then turned back to me, worry drawing his face taut.

"I'll be all right," I told him.

He placed his fingertips to his mouth, kissed them and held up his hand, palm out. I kissed my fingers and did the same. Our hands passed through one another's.

He winked at me, mischievous to the end, then turned to Tommy. His lips formed the word "Go".

And then he was gone.

Tommy grabbed my hand and led me through the garden. I could hardly make out where I stepped through the stream of my tears, but Tommy gently guided me through the brambles and shadows.

"Nobody's here!" came a shout from the kitchen.

"They've gone!"

"But I saw a pistol with no one holding it."

"That busy imagination of yours at work again, Bran." The man's laughter filtered out to us on the breeze.

"Hey there!" someone shouted. "You there. Dawson, that you? Did you see the gypsies?"

"They left some time ago," Tommy called back without breaking his stride.

"Where's your friend, the big fellow with the sword?"

"Gone home."

Home. But Purgatory was no home for a good soul. Quin didn't belong there. But he didn't belong here, either.

* * *

I DECIDED to remain at Freak House a little longer. I couldn't leave the one place where I felt close to Quin. The portal at the ruins might bring horrors and danger, but it also linked Quin to this realm. I stopped short of hoping a demon infestation would be unleashed just so he would return. I desperately wanted to see him, but not if it meant others would be put in harm's way.

Jack and Hannah returned from London, bringing Samuel and Charity with them. It felt good to have my friends close. I missed Emily and Jacob immensely, but I didn't want to darken their summer with my melancholia.

Their children deserved a happy, fun aunt, not a gloomy one.

"You must come for a walk," Charity said, sitting beside me on the ruined abbey wall. She removed the book from my hands and snapped it shut. I'd been stuck on the same page for an hour.

"It might rain." I looked up at the sky. Not a single cloud marred the blue expanse.

Hannah took my hand. "Come on. You have to do something. You've been sitting on this wall pretending to read for three days now."

He's not coming back. She didn't need to say it, but I heard it nevertheless.

I sighed. "I don't feel like walking."

"You don't feel like anything much, of late."

Charity patted my hand and gave me a sympathetic look. "Nobody expects you to simply forget and suddenly be happy again. We just want you to get some exercise for your health."

Exercise wouldn't mend my broken heart. But she was trying—they both were—and deserved my thanks if nothing else.

Hannah's eyes twinkled. "If you don't wish to walk, we could go for a swim in the lake instead."

"Hannah!" Charity stared at her. "We don't have any bathing costumes."

"We can wear our shifts. Come on. The day is warm and nobody will see us."

"Unless they look out of one of the windows, or venture over from the drive."

"Cara?"

I shrugged. "I don't feel up to much frivolity today." Or any other day.

"It might help you get your mind off...your sorrows."

Hannah's smile turned sympathetic. "If only for a few minutes."

Charity stepped back and gave a decisive nod. "You're right. If Cara goes in, then so will I."

Hannah grinned. "Now you *have* to, Cara. Wouldn't you love to see the prim future Mrs. Samuel Gladstone take a dip in her shift?"

"I am not prim!"

I smiled at Charity's protest. It was the first one I'd mustered since Quin left.

"Perhaps not," Hannah said to Charity, "but you are annoyingly perfect. I would like to see your hair a bedraggled mess once in a while."

Charity removed the pins from her hair and shook the blonde tresses out. It cascaded over her shoulders like a beautiful pale waterfall. Then she kicked off her shoes and removed her stockings. Hannah laughed and followed suit.

"Should we see if Sylvia wants to join us?" I asked them, removing my ankle boots.

"Charity's primness is nothing compared to Sylvia's," Hannah said. "She would have a fit if she knew."

"I am *not* prim." To prove it, Charity was the first one in. She walked right up to the edge and kept on walking. "It's a little cold. And the bottom squelches." She turned to us as the water reached her thighs, her eyes bright with laughter. "But it's rather refreshing."

"Besides," Hannah went on, "Sylvia will be too busy sneaking around the house with Tommy. I hear the tower room is their favorite venue for rendezvous these days." She removed her dress and corset and laid it over the wall. Then she plunged into the lake, up to her neck. She beckoned me to follow.

"They'd better hope her uncle doesn't find out," Charity said as I undressed.

"You think he'll be angry?" I asked. "Won't he be pleased that she's happy? Tommy is a wonderful fellow."

Charity sighed as I came up beside her. The water was indeed cool, but invigorating at the same time. We both walked further in to where Hannah paddled. The mud on the bottom changed to sand and the water turned clearer.

"He is," Hannah said. "But he's not the man August wants her to be with."

"*He* shouldn't talk," I said. "His choice of lover is not exactly conventional."

They stared at me, probably surprised that I'd worked out what Bollard meant to Langley.

"Try telling that to August." Hannah floated on her back, propelling herself by flapping her hands through the water like fins. "He wouldn't accept Tommy in a million years. I'm afraid, if she insists, we're in for an unhappy time of it."

Charity sighed again. "This is all so sad. I only want everyone to be happy. I like to see laughter, not tears."

"I know how to make at least one person laugh." Hannah had that twinkle in her eyes again. I edged away from her.

"Oh?" Charity blinked innocently. "Who? And how?"

Hannah swooshed her hand through the water, soaking Charity. Charity gasped and coughed, but both Hannah and I laughed. The perfect, poised Charity Evans was wet through, her hair a dripping mop.

Charity quickly recovered and splashed Hannah back. I whooped, earning me a splash from both of them. We kicked and flicked water over one another until we were all breathing heavily and soaked to the bone. Then we collapsed in giggles until Hannah's smile faded, her gaze on the house.

"Something's wrong." She stood and the water cascaded off her. "Sylvia's running."

We waded out of the lake and met Sylvia in the ruins near

our clothes. She pressed her hand to her heaving chest as she gulped in large breaths.

"Sylvia!" I cried. "What is it? Is someone hurt?"

She shook her head, sending her curls into a mad dance around her temples. "You must come back to the house. All of you. Oh, God, it's awful. Just awful."

It must indeed be bad if she made not a single comment about the three of us dressed in nothing but our shifts and swimming in the lake where any visitor could see us.

"Sylvia!" Hannah grabbed her cousin by the shoulders and shook her. Sylvia began to cry. "Tell us what happened."

"He saw us."

"Who saw who doing what?"

"Uncle August," she sobbed. "He saw Tommy and me... kissing. Oh why oh why didn't we go to the tower room?"

Charity put her arm around Sylvia's shoulders. "Calm down. It'll be all right. Jack will speak to—"

"Jack has tried!" She buried her face in her hands and sobbed. "He's sending him away. Uncle is banishing Tommy."

I gasped and exchanged glances with the other two. "Are you certain?"

"Of course I'm certain." She looked at me, but I doubted she saw me very well through her tears. "He told him to pack his bags and leave today. Immediately!"

"But where will he go?" Charity asked. "What will he do?"

"I don't know!" Sylvia wailed. "What can he do with only one functioning arm? He's unfit to work as a footman or butler, and he's qualified for nothing else."

"And Langley won't give him a reference," Hannah said quietly.

That only made Sylvia cry harder. "He can't go! Nobody will take him on! He'll end up in the poor house! Or back on the streets!"

"It won't be as bad as that," Charity soothed. "Jack will see that he's taken care of."

"And what of his pride? Hmmm? Will Jack see that he retains that too?"

"This isn't right." Hannah gathered up her clothes and snatched up her shoes. "Not after everything Tommy's done for us." She stormed off through the ruins toward the house.

"Where are you going?" Charity called after her.

"To have a word with August. He must be made to see reason."

"But you can't! You're wet." Sylvia frowned at Charity and me as if she'd just noticed that we too were wet. "Did you all fall into the lake?"

"Something like that." Charity put her gown on over the top of her wet shift and collected her boots. "Come on. Let's sort this out." She gathered Sylvia into her arms. "It'll be all right. You'll see."

Sylvia sighed. "I do hope so." She took my hand. "Come on, Cara."

"It's not really my affair." I wasn't sure I wanted to become embroiled in Sylvia's drama. I had enough misery of my own to weigh me down.

"It is! You're as much a part of this family as anyone. You and Charity. Besides, it might provide some distraction for your thoughts so they don't continue to return to Quin."

Mention of him brought the tears close again. I hid them by putting my gown on and tightening the laces at the front. When I finished, Sylvia took one hand and Charity the other.

"I miss him," I said simply.

Charity squeezed my hand. "We know."

I drew in a deep breath and walked with them back to the house.

NOW AVAILABLE

MY SOUL TO TAKE
The third book in the THIRD FREAK HOUSE TRILOGY.

When Myer returns through the portal and brings Quin's nemesis with him, Cara and Quin are reunited again. Only to be ripped apart by a villain who has been playing a long game. Can they ever be together in this realm? The final novel in the Freak House series will be the most heart-stopping yet.

Subscribe to C.J's newsletter to get exclusive access to a Freak House story. Sign up at www.cjarcher.com

A MESSAGE FROM THE AUTHOR

I hope you enjoyed reading this book as much as I enjoyed writing it. As an independent author, getting the word out about my book is vital to its success, so if you liked this book please consider telling your friends and writing a review at the store where you purchased it. If you would like to be contacted when I release a new book, subscribe to my newsletter at http://cjarcher.com/contact-cj/newsletter/. You will only be contacted when I have a new book out.

ALSO BY C.J. ARCHER

SERIES WITH 2 OR MORE BOOKS

The Glass Library

Cleopatra Fox Mysteries

After The Rift

Glass and Steele

The Ministry of Curiosities Series

The Emily Chambers Spirit Medium Trilogy

The 1st Freak House Trilogy

The 2nd Freak House Trilogy

The 3rd Freak House Trilogy

The Assassins Guild Series

Lord Hawkesbury's Players Series

Witch Born

SINGLE TITLES NOT IN A SERIES

Courting His Countess

Surrender

Redemption

The Mercenary's Price

ABOUT THE AUTHOR

C.J. Archer has loved history and books for as long as she can remember and feels fortunate that she found a way to combine the two. She spent her early childhood in the dramatic beauty of outback Queensland, Australia, but now lives in suburban Melbourne with her husband, two children and a mischievous black & white cat named Coco.

Subscribe to C.J.'s newsletter through her website to be notified when she releases a new book, as well as get access to exclusive content and subscriber-only giveaways. Her website also contains up to date details on all her books: http://cjarcher.com She loves to hear from readers. You can contact her through email cj@cjarcher.com or follow her on social media to get the latest updates on her books:

facebook.com/CJArcherAuthorPage

x.com/cj_archer

instagram.com/authorcjarcher

bookbub.com/authors/c-j-archer

9 780992 583460